He Touched Me

He Touched Me

SHEILAH R. CRAFT

STARLIGHT Books

STARLIGHT BOOKS

STARLIGHT BOOKS

STARLIGHT Books

DEDICATED TO

ELVIS AARON PRESLEY—

THANK YOU FOR THE

GREATEST GIFT

Do not stand at my grave and weep
I am not there. I do not sleep.
I am a thousand winds that blow.
I am the diamond glints on snow.
I am the sunlight on ripened grain.
I am the gentle autumn rain.
When you awaken in the morning's hush
I am the swift uplifting rush
Of quiet birds in circled flight.
I am the soft stars that shine at night.
Do not stand at my grave and cry;
I am not there. I did not die.

--Mary Elizabeth Frye

CONTENTS

AUTHOR'S NOTE

Writing stories is nothing new or unusual for me. I wrote my first, albeit simple, story when I was a toddler. The writing process—from inception of plot and characters to completion—is always easy for me. I am never plagued by this thing most people label writer's block. When the ideas fill my brain and the characters come to life, I have all I need to plow through the process relatively quickly. I'm not bragging, just explaining my writing.

I do become quite emotionally invested in each novel I write, living through the events and moments with the people (characters). That very often is emotionally and physically draining. However, writing becomes cathartic for me as well, allowing me to purge pain or grief or guilt and to heal. That happened with each of the six *Heart-Glow* novels I've written.

Those novels of course are inspired and influenced by my life experiences, but they are not autobiographical. Neither is *He Touched Me*. Rather, this novella is my "what if" scenario. Yes, I lived through the 1970s. I fell in love with Elvis when I heard him while I was in my mother's womb. I've never stopped loving and admiring him.

I was blessed to attend his June 26, 1977 concert at Market Square Arena in Indianapolis, literally my life's dream come true. My world crumbled on the afternoon of August 16, just weeks after that spectacular concert. I had spent the nights of 1975 onward praying for God to heal Elvis and to take care of him.

I gave a lot of my emotions, thoughts, and experiences to Caroline Hart, whose dreams-come-true are more than my young self ever dared to dream. Caroline gets to do what I wish I had been able to do—befriend and attempt to help this extraordinary and complex man.

This historical novella combines my perspective and experiences with Elvis Presley's life, combined with a dose of imagination to create a believable and touching story.

My goal is to honor the man who did touch my life and influence it for the better. In that vein, I will donate 5% of my royalties from sales of *He Touched Me* to St. Jude Children's Research Hospital in Elvis's name, continuing his legendary philanthropy.

PRELUDE:
BECAUSE OF LOVE

*J*une 3, 1973

Well, I am on a journey to manifest my dream, the dream that has consumed my brain since I was four years old. Most people would tell me that my dream is childish, impossible, perhaps foolish, or even improbable. I don't care. This is my dream, and I have to try to make it come true.

I have been on this Greyhound bus for just over two and a half hours, and I will arrive in Memphis around 7:00 tomorrow morning. I have everything planned. I will get a motel room, and take my chances outside his gates like so many people do. Seeing him is part of the dream, of course, but the most important part to me is telling him what he has done to me and for me.

No, I have never met him, and I do not personally know him, but I do love him. There is so much about him that I respect and strive to aspire toward: philanthropy, compassion, charity, generosity, strong faith, and abiding love of God. More than any person I know or know about, this one man has affected, influenced, and changed me more than anyone else ever could.

It's important for me that he knows all he has done for someone he never met. I don't mean to be sacrilegious, but in that respect he is as close to God as I will ever get on this earth. No, he is not God or a god; he is a man, but not an ordinary man. This man has been touched by God. This man has a far greater purpose than most of us who walk this planet. This man is one of God's agents, with the mission to do what he has done for me—to save lives.

This man saved me. Without knowing it, this man helped me find my life's purpose so that I can do and be all that God intends for me. Without this man, I would be adrift, with no defined purpose and no intimate relationship with God.

More than any one person, he touched me. He touched me as no other ever can.

VERSE ONE:
LET'S BE FRIENDS

I watched him as he walked toward me. The dozens of people walking or driving nearby stopped and stared at him. Who wouldn't? This man was different. First of all, he was quite tall, over six feet. He was surrounded by an aura of prominence. He resembled Adonis come to life. His pure black hair and sideburns were perfectly coiffed. His Grecian nose and full lips were flawlessly formed. His high cheekbones indicated Native American ancestry, as did his olive complexion. He looked straight ahead, although I couldn't see his eyes due to his gold aviator-style sunglasses. His outfit and accessories could not be ignored, and they definitely set him apart from all others.

He wore a black crushed-velvet suit with a white silk shirt. I could see a diamond cross and a golden chai exposed against the skin of his upper chest where his shirt was unbuttoned. Gold and gemstone rings bedecked his fingers, eight in total. As he walked with his assured and determined stroll, his black leather boot heels resounded on the concrete sidewalk. In his left hand he held an onyx walking stick topped by a pure silver tiger head.

He was the one most beautiful human being I had ever seen—in movies, in photographs, in art, or in the flesh. But why was he walking down the sidewalk like a normal pedestrian? Sure, he was a man, but he was as far from normal as anyone could ever get. I stared as he neared me, and I felt my heart pounding and making me lightheaded. He never saw me. I was probably one foot shorter than he, and with his straightforward gaze, I was not in his line of vision. Suddenly, my entire body shook with the force of the impact. Everything was dark for several moments.

I heard that voice, the one I had heard numerous times in movies, on television, or on records. Was I dreaming? I slowly opened my eyes, and saw him cradling me. His eyes, those eyes. Those deep blue eyes looked at me in concern as that velvety Southern voice asked, "Are you all right, honey?"

Of course I was all right. I was in the arms of the most magnetic, most powerful, most magnificent man to ever live. I had come to Memphis dreaming to see him. Who said dreams don't come true? I thought as I nodded my head and felt my heart pound again when he smiled that curled-lip smile at me.

"Can you stand?" he asked me. I nodded, still staring at him. "Are you sure?" I nodded again, and he smiled. "All right. You hold on to me, and I'll help you."

I grasped his arms, and he slowly pulled me to my feet. I still looked up at him, stunned and mesmerized. My head seem to swirl as I attempted to discern reality from dream.

"Whoa, steady there. I'm sorry, darlin'. I never saw you. I sure never meant to hurt you."

"No. It was my fault. I-I should have moved. I saw you. I'm fine," I managed to say.

"I'm not so sure. I'm going to take you home and have my doctor check you over," he insisted. "Joe, bring the car." Home? His home? Graceland? This had to be a dream. I felt lightheaded again, and felt his arm around me. "You landed on the sidewalk hard. You could have hit your head. No walking until the all-clear from Dr. Nick."

Before I could fully process everything, he picked me up and carried me in his arms. Soon he seated me on the plush leather seat of a red and black Lincoln Mark IV. I had seen pictures of him driving this car. Now I was seated next to him in the car. The day had become surreal, and even though I could hear him and feel him, I wasn't convinced I wasn't having a hallucination.

When the car entered those gates—the music note gates—and dozens of people screamed his name or took his picture, I wasn't convinced. When he lifted me in his arms and carried me into his living room, I still wasn't convinced. But when he placed me on the long white sofa, I snapped out of my confusion and leapt to my feet.

He and his friends looked at me in bcfuddlement. "Joe, did you call Nick?" he quickly, urgently asked.

"Yes. He's on his way," Joe reassured.

"Come on, now, you just lie down here until the doctor arrives," he urged, concern evident in his voice.

"No, I can't." The men each furrowed their brows. "I'll get your sofa dirty," I explained.

"Is that what this is about?" he asked with a smile. "Lie down. There is nothing to worry about, I promise."

Just then, Dr. Nichopoulos entered the living room, and forced the issue. He leaned me back on the couch, shined a light in my eyes, and felt my head and neck. "I'm fine," I insisted, only to have him shush me.

"You have a nasty bump on your head. It could be a concussion, but it's too soon to tell. You need to stay awake for twenty-four hours as a precaution. Do you have someone who can make sure you don't fall asleep?"

Of course I didn't. I had left my family's home two days before and come to Memphis. I hadn't met anyone yet except him, but. . . . Should I lie and get myself out of this? I couldn't involve him any longer.

"Yeah, sure she does. She can keep me company tonight."

I was hallucinating again. Had he just said that? I heard his friends moan and grumble. I sat up and said I would be fine in my motel room. "I can't force myself on your kindness any longer."

"Nonsense. You're not forcing yourself. Far from it. I can't make you stay? Why?"

My heart pounded. This was a dream come true, but I refused to take advantage of him. "You are as kind and benevolent as I knew you are, but I can't impose on you. I won't take advantage of your kindness any longer. Thank you for everything."

I took a few steps, heading toward the front door, when I felt a strong hand on my arm. It's not that I really wanted to leave, but I did refuse to exploit the accident. I had seen him, touched him, talked with him, and been inside his famous home. Heck, I had even been knocked to the ground by him. What more could I expect?

"Where are you going?"

"My motel room," I mumbled.

"And how do you expect to get there? Walk?" I nodded. He started to retort, but Dr. Nichopoulos spoke first.

"No. I don't advise that at all. If you do have a concussion, the risks are too great. Where is your family?"

I had no choice but to tell them. "Philadelphia," I whispered.

"That settles it. Conversation all night. Come with me, Little Bit; we're going to the TV room."

I was too overwhelmed by all that had happened to protest. Besides, I never wanted to hurt his feelings, and it seemed that my continued reluctance would do just that. He carried me down the stairs, and then helped me settle on the sofa.

"What is your name Little Bit? I'm Elvis Presley."

Had he just introduced himself, as if I had no idea who he was? "I know," I forced myself to respond. "Everyone knows about you." He smiled and looked down, as if embarrassed. "I'm Caroline Hart."

He quickly looked up with a smile. "Sweet Caroline. . .," he sang. My heart pounded yet again, and I felt tears threatening me.

"Hey why the tears? Are you sick? Or is my singing that bad?" He winked, so I knew he was teasing. I shook my head. "Then what?"

"Everything." I took a deep breath and relaxed myself as much as I could. "Everything that's happened this evening. It's all so much, and I'm overwhelmed by it all." He looked at me expectantly, waiting for me to continue. "I came here because of you. I wrote you a letter six months ago, but you get so much mail that I never expected you to ever see it. But there is so much that I want you to know. I never actually thought I would ever meet you, but I did think that perhaps if I wrote another letter and gave it to the guard at your gates, it might get to you. I know I sound crazy. I'm sorry. I really wasn't stalking you. I had no idea you'd be on that street. You really took me by surprise."

"We had to buy something at one of the stores there. I bought a few more things while I was there. We were on our way to the car when I ran into you," he smiled. "So what is so important that you came all the way to Memphis to tell me?"

This was it. This was the chance for which I had dreamed and prayed. I looked into his eyes and spoke from my heart. "You changed my life completely. Oh, I know thousands of people say that, and I know they all mean it. But no one on this earth has affected me as you have. I have long seen and felt how strong your faith is, and how much you love Jesus. That had a huge impact on me since I was four.

"It's not that my family isn't Christian. They are. My parents and grandparents all are. It's just that you, well, you touch my heart in a way no one else ever has. Or rather, the Lord's word touches me through you." He stared at me with tears filling his eyes. "One morning, it was a Monday, before I left for school, I sat on my bed and listened to your gospel music. I picked up my Bible and read from I Corinthians. Something happened that I don't know if I can explain. I suddenly felt lighter and happier than ever, and calmer, too. As I was listening to you sing *He Touched Me*, I felt God touch me. He came to me. He changed me. He saved me. I was twelve years old.

"Ever since then, I have not been tempted by Satan to slip into sin. I am not short-tempered or angry. I really don't let everyday stuff bother me. I am more patient and kind toward others. Everyone who knew me then noticed the change in me.

"I know God is the one who changed and saved me really, but I know it's because of you, because of your example and passion. I owe you more than I could ever repay." I stared deep into his eyes, his soul, as I continued. "You are my bell-sheep, the one who guided me, beckoned me, closer to God. You helped me to see the most important truth—that a relationship with God is the most meaningful relationship I can have. Because of you, I prayed to God to forgive me for my sins. He did, and I was reborn. Your testimony saved me."

I paused and studied his face, his reaction. His eyes were still tear-filled, but he was smiling. I wanted to tell him more, certain that this would be my only chance to do so. "This really all started when I was seven and saw *Wild in the Country*. That scene when your character is asked what Jesus said on the cross, and you say it in Aramaic with all of the passion of Jesus, really made me think about what Jesus did for me. Sunday school teachers had talked about it, and so did the minister, but the depth of emotion and truth that came through you really affected me.

"So did Dr. John Carpenter. I saw that film the first day it was released four years ago. In fact, I sat through every showing for the first weekend, November 15 and 16. That movie really changed my life."

"*Change of Habit?* Really? Most people don't take it too seriously. How?"

"Because of how you portrayed John Carpenter, brought him to life. I know other people wrote the screenplay and created the story and characters, but actors bring life to the characters. John Carpenter is a testimony himself—a man living in the secular world, who is already living by many of God's virtues and commandments: helping people, caring for them, and without pay. That sort of man is kind, compassionate, humble, and unselfish. Just like you are. That's why John Carpenter evokes those virtues—you imbue him with them. In many ways, he is you. That movie made me want to become a social worker. I want to help people like you and John Carpenter do. As a child of God, I don't have to become a nun. I can still live in the secular world, live by God's word, and help people. That's what I want to do, that's what I feel called to do."

He bowed his head for several moments, then looked at me and grasped my hand. "I-I don't know what to say. No one has ever told me anything like this before. When I was a child I knew there had to be a reason I was alive, why I was born. I didn't know what for a long time. But then I realized my purpose is to be an entertainer and to make people happy. That's all. Don't give me credit I don't deserve, Little Bit."

"I'm not. Yes, God gifted you with this amazing voice for a reason. Yes, you do make people happy, but there's much more to this. God has a grander purpose for you than just rock music."

"Like what? How do you know?" He looked confused, his brow furrowed.

"Rock brought you fame, worldwide fame, and with it a global audience. God used the rock and roll for that reason mostly, besides that it makes people feel good. You've long said gospel is your favorite music, and that you wanted to join a gospel quartet, right?" He nodded. "You sang your first professional gospel song to the nation on live TV in 1956. No one expected that, right? The boy who people had labeled the antichrist showed his love of God on live TV, with many thousands of people watching. You changed people's minds, probably some of those screaming teens'. Then came the gospel albums and singles. You did become a gospel singer, and your gospel is heard by millions of people all over the world. How many people came to know God through your records? For how many other people were you the bell-sheep? You have affected and changed many lives, just as you did mine."

He was quiet and thoughtful for a few minutes, but then grabbed my hands and held them close to him. "This is the most beautiful thing anyone has ever said to me or about me. I led you to God? Well that's-that's more than my mind can comprehend. I-I don't know what to say. I just live my life. I never did anything that would displease my parents, especially my mother. I was raised in the church, and God has always been important to me. I know I've done some things to displease Him, but I've talked with Him. I've done my best to follow His commandments and to live by His word, but I know I fall short. I'm ashamed of myself for that."

"No, don't be. We all make mistakes, all of us. I've done some things in the past that I'm not proud of, but I talk with God, too, and I plead for His forgiveness. I've slid backwards and done some of those things again, and it made me feel just horrible. At first I was afraid to go to God again, afraid He would deny me. Then I read some Scriptures and knew He wouldn't do that. He won't do that to anyone who asks in faith and true desire to change and for forgiveness."

I knew he had gone through very painful situations like the death of his mother and the breakup of his marriage. I also felt it in my heart that there were health issues, too. Don't ask me how, but I just knew. I had something else to tell him, so I took a deep breath. "I pray for you every day, for your well-being and your peace. I wasn't going to say anything to you, but somehow it was placed on my heart to pray for your health. So I do, every day. I have faith that God will do what is best for you, I do." I held his hand tightly, overtaken by my emotions. I couldn't stop the tears from sliding down my cheeks.

Suddenly, I felt his soft fingers brushing them away. "Hush. Don't cry for me, Little Bit." He wrapped his arms around me, pulled me close to him, and shushed me gently. I could feel and hear his heart beating, and the feeling soothed me. I stopped crying, dried my eyes, and sat up, looking into his eyes. Before I could say anything, he spoke.

"Yeah, Little Bit, this body is not what it used to be. But I do what I have to do to get by, to keep going. I'm supporting a lot of people, you know. I do some things I shouldn't, but if I didn't,

I couldn't do all of this. Each of us has a cross to bear, just like Jesus did. Nothing I go through can compare to what He went through, but it's tough. We all have things we have to deal with. Some of us do a better job than others," he said and smiled. "But I talk with God a lot, and tell Him what's going on and why I do what I do. I know He knows all, but I like to tell Him. It makes me feel closer to Him."

I nodded. "Yes, I know that, too. I can tell."

"How?"

"When I listen to your gospel songs, I can hear your love for God the Father and Jesus the Son. I can hear it, your belief, conviction, faith, love. I can feel it, almost literally. It goes to my core. You do what the Bible tells us to do. You profess your faith when you sing. You glorify God when you sing. You let people know your relationship with God and Jesus when you sing. You evangelize when you sing, just as the apostles did when they taught people about Jesus.

"You know, I even feel it in a lot of your secular music, too. When I first heard *The Wonder of You*, I told my dad you were singing to God. This wasn't a love song to a woman. It was a love song to God."

His smile was huge. "That's exactly what it was, Little Bit. I told my wife that then. Yeah, I can have fun with some of the music, but for me, a lot of the songs have a deeper meaning that most people don't pick up on. Here you are, this little slip of a girl, and you know me better than some people who've known me for years. How old are you?"

"Nineteen."

"You're wise beyond your years, Little Bit. I have something I want to show you. I'll be back in a few minutes."

I sat on the sofa, not daring to move and look around. I had intruded enough. I did, of course, glance around, just awestruck at all that had happened. Even in my dreams, nothing like sitting in his home, alone with him, ever happened. I was snapped back to reality when I heard his footsteps on the stairs.

He sat facing me, two books in his hands. The largest, obviously his Bible, was well-worn. I could tell how often he read it. He opened the Bible to Psalms and turned it toward me. Psalms 149:5 was underlined. In the space between Psalms and Proverbs, he had written *SING FOR THE GLORY OF GOD.* I stared at the page for what felt like days. Emotions surged through me, engulfed me. I finally looked at him and managed to choke out, "That's what you do."

Without saying anything, he placed his Bible in my hands. He opened the smaller book, scanning it for a specific page. I saw the title. *The Prophet*, one of his favorite books. He found what he was seeking and put the book in my hand. At the bottom of page 39, he had written *God loves you but he loves you best when you sing.*

"God loves you tremendously," I whispered as I stared at the page. "You glorify Him constantly. He gifted you your incredible voice, and you use this gift to bring joy to people. But you also honor God and Jesus with your singing. What more could He want from you? Your faith is strong, you accept Jesus as your Savior, and you evangelize and honor God. Plus, you're compassionate and generous—charity, the love in the Bible. These are all that really matter as long as you are right with God."

"Yeah, I know, Little Bit. I sure do look forward to Heaven, to meeting Jesus and to seeing my mother again. I sure do miss her. I could have used her advice over the past fifteen years, I really could. But what's done is done, and I can't change anything. As David said, *'thy will be done.'* God does things His way, whether we like it or not. He thinks it's for the best, and I suppose it is. I love Him, even though I struggle."

I sat, stunned. He had shared his innermost thoughts and feelings with me. I felt honored, privileged. I was. "This world, this path you are placed on, is too much for someone like you. You must feel the weight of the universe crushing you. It's because you pick up all of the energies around you, the thoughts, concerns, illnesses of people, even strangers. A packed arena, with several thousand people, must overload your soul. That's an awful lot for one man to carry," I responded.

"You are an empath, someone who does just that—pick up the energies, thoughts, issues of other people. It's a heavy burden."

"There is a name for that?" he asked. "I never understood what that was, what was happening to me. Tell me more," he requested.

"You are very sensitive to the emotional experiences of people and animals. Even places. You sense what's inside people. But you also pick up on tone of voice, body language, movements, the words they use or avoid, their logical process, and what they hide from the world. Nothing is hidden from you, from an empath. There are probably times you go off, freak out, for no reason it seems like. Then you learn that someone close to you went through something, like an injury or even stress.

"You are always overrun by outside emotions, those that aren't yours, and they make it seem like you can't figure out why you feel that way. There is no way you can resolve or deal with those emotions, because they aren't yours. You can have a very hard time figuring out what you really feel or what you get from others."

He shook his head. "This is all beginning to make sense. I felt that since I was a young little boy, and I thought something was wrong with me. This is a lot to take in."

"There's more," I added.

"Like what?"

"Well, the emotions come together in you in a force, in a way that gives you God-like powers. You absorb negative emotions of other people, in your body, physically take those emotions. This can often manifest, and make you physically sick.

"You were born in empath. You were an empath before you were born, when you existed as a soul in Heaven. You embody God's virtues. You are so incredibly caring and loving that you almost always put others before yourself. You invest your energies in taking care of others, but you don't take care of yourself. I know why." Tears filled my eyes again as I looked at this gorgeous being. To me, his physical beauty mirrored his soul's beauty, so much so that I often became inundated with emotions just looking at an album cover.

"More? What else could there be?"

I turned to Hebrews 1:14 in his Bible, gave it to him, and told him to read it. He did, aloud in that voice. "'*Are they not all ministering spirits sent out to serve for the sake of those who are to inherit salvation.*' God sends His angels to earth, yeah, I believe that. God wants us to treat everyone we meet with kindness, because we don't know who might be one of his angels. For all I know, you're an angel, Little Bit."

"No, I'm not. You are."

"Me? An angel? You can't be. . . . You are serious, aren't you?"

"Yes, I am. That's why you don't always feel like you belong here and now. You come from a very different, very calm place. Earth is too chaotic and cruel for an angel. It's all too much, out of the norm, for you. But this world is part of your purpose, your mission."

"How-how do you know I feel out of place a lot of the time, like I don't belong? How could you know that?" He stared at me intently, his eyes pleading with me. "And, what mission?"

"To lead people to God, what I was talking about before. God is using you, His beautiful, talented angel, to change people's hearts. Through you, people learn more about God and let Him into their hearts. That's what happened to me. Because of you, I am saved and reborn. Because of God working through you," I told him, all of my love evident in my voice. "Your entire life on earth is for this purpose. It's just so very sad that the one who brings so much happiness and the path to salvation suffers so much. I pray you don't."

"But an angel? Me? That's way too-too high for me," he protested. "Little Bit, don't exalt me so. God is the one you should exalt."

"I do, Mr. Presley. I give God the credit and glory for all that has happened to me, my rebirth, and salvation. But that does not mean I can't acknowledge the truth about you, too. What I know and said about you isn't wrong in any sense. It's not wrong for me to know it and to tell it. And it's not incorrect. It's true."

"How do you know this, Little Bit? How?"

"God revealed it to me in a dream. Earlier this year, I prayed my evening prayer to God. I always ask for my continued salvation and wisdom, my parents' faith and salvation, and for you, your health, well-being, and protection. I got in bed, and I fell asleep. I vividly remember the dream I had. I saw you in Heaven with a very beautiful being. Michael, the Archangel, was telling you what you were to do: go to earth as a newborn infant and live the life God assigned for you. Your purpose was told to you. You would be given talents by God, and you were to use those gifts. Michael told you to honor God in your work and tell people about God. Then you disappeared from Heaven. After you had gone, Michael smiled and whispered, '*You will do many great things in God's name, my brother. I will meet you again someday.*' I wrote the dream in my diary the next day.

"I also prayed to God for Him to tell me somehow if the dream was true and from Him or not. For the next six nights, I had the exact same dream—for one week. The eighth morning, still lying in my bed, I asked God once more if the dream was from Him or if Satan was tempting me. I had to know. That second, your song *Let Us Pray* sounded in my room. My radio's batteries were dead, and there were no records on my turntable. So I knew God was causing me to hear that song. It's one of my very favorites. I knew the truth about you, straight from God.”

“I-I believe you, Little Bit, I do. But how come I don’t remember any of this? I mean, it happened to me, so why haven’t I ever remembered this?”

I shook my head and admitted, “I don’t know. All I know is that God let me know it’s true. Why he chose me to reveal this to is a mystery to me, unless it’s because I feel so very strongly about you.”

“Then my running into you this evening was no accident. We were brought together. Divine providence. God did this; he lined up all the pieces for us to meet. I believe that. I’m sorry you got hurt, though, but I guess He knew that was the only way for us to come together.”

He looked at the Bible in his hands. “Everything you’ve told me is very heavy, hard to digest. But I believe it, all of it. Don’t ask me why. I can’t explain it, but I feel it. I feel the truth in you. We just met, but you don’t feel like a stranger to me. And the weird thing is, I feel totally comfortable and safe telling you all of this. I don’t open up to people easily, never have," he said and smiled like a little boy.

He reminded me of a little boy—alone and uncertain. He came across differently to many people, so confident and secure, but I saw him as the shy, sheltered boy from Tupelo. And I knew that his mother's death still devastated him. He had done all of it—the home, the cars, being the sole support—for his parents, particularly his mother. He knew she was safe and loved in Heaven, but that didn't fully heal his wound. I stared into his eyes as I thought about this angelic being who had suffered so on this earth.

"We all suffer, Little Bit; everyone who lives on this planet suffers. That's the price we pay for the original sin. Each person has their own cross to bear, just as Jesus carried the cross on which he was murdered. I'm no different from anyone else. My blood is red, my body has its issues, and I feel every emotion known to man. I get angry. I have a temper. I sometimes say things I shouldn't. I'm far from perfect, so don't make me perfect in your mind and your heart. I'll only end up breaking your heart if you do."

I felt flabbergasted. "How did you know what I was thinking?" I knew the answer as soon as I asked the question. "You read my thoughts. I read about Michael and the other Archangels. They can read people's thoughts. Other angels must be able to also."

He grinned. "Or maybe it's part of that empath stuff you were talking about."

"Maybe," I agreed. I realized how discomfiting this was for him, so I changed the subject. "One of my favorite chapters is Psalm 139. I try to read it every morning. It lets me know that God has always known me from the moment He created my soul. He knows everything I've thought, done, and said, but more than that, he knows my heart. He knows the real me. I like that," I said with a smile.

He also smiled. "I like that one, too. God made me, and He understands me. When I slip, and I do, He forgives me. He's my Father, and He loves me like a good parent, and He forgives. I won't say His love is unconditional, 'cause He lets us know His conditions in this book." He held up his Bible. "It's our duty to know His conditions and to follow His word in this Bible. If we do, and if we believe that Jesus is God's Son and died for us, then we are God's children. Isn't that awesome?"

"Yes, it really is," I softly said. He spoke with the passion of an apostle, and my emotions were engulfed in an ocean of intensity that I had never felt.

"You know, Larry is probably the only other person I've talked to about anything like this. It feels good, Little Bit. I mean, I talk to God, but that's just between me and Him. But it's good to talk with other believers. None of us can go on this journey alone. Fellowship is important, God tells us. So I need this. We all need this."

"No one I know wants to talk about God and Scripture, not really," I said. "They tolerate me to a point, but I can tell they don't want to get into it. I don't know why. I mean, the Bible is our guidebook to life; it teaches how we're supposed to live. I can't imagine not being saved and living a life without God. Why would anyone want to risk their eternity?"

He shook his head. "I don't know; I really don't. For me, I know I wouldn't sing the way I do if it weren't for God, so why wouldn't I want to use my voice for Him as well as for other people's entertainment? I owe Him everything. I mean, He gave it to me. He can take it all away if I offend Him."

"How could you ever offend God?" The thought had never occurred to me. How could it? Yes, I had read the tales of drug use, but I also knew that there were indeed serious health issues. What exactly, I didn't know, but I knew a person whose pain couldn't be controlled by what her doctors prescribed. In her agony, she sought other medications that could help her, medications not authorized by her doctor. I explained this to Elvis, and he asked if it was a school friend of mine.

"No. She's my mother." His shock was evident. "Her doctor sent her to several specialists, but none can find anything wrong with her. She's in constant pain, and no one can tell her why. Three of the doctors told her it was psychosomatic, but it's not. I've seen her crying in pain. So what was she supposed to do? She couldn't function. So my parents found a doctor who will give her pain pills. It's not perfect, but she's not curled in a crying ball most of the time."

He asked what kind of pain, and the look in his eyes told me he, too, suffered from chronic pain. "It's really everywhere," I said. "Her arms, wrists, legs, knees, back, neck, headaches. It's constant, but it changes frequently. She also has trouble sleeping since this started, and she's exhausted all the time, like she's drained of energy. It all just started a few years ago and won't stop."

"Well, that's tough Little Bit. I'm so sorry. Let's say a prayer for her healing. Give me your hands." I placed my hands in his and bowed my head. "Oh, God, we pray for Mrs. Hart's healing. Lift her up in your blessings. Anoint her with strength and healing. With one touch you alone can stop her pain and make her whole. This we ask of you, our loving and merciful God. We trust you, the best physician. We know that you can heal Mrs. Hart if that is your will. Amen."

I repeated Amen and looked at him with deeper love and respect. I knew how much he suffered, but he put others before himself. I silently prayed for his healing in that moment.

While he still held my hands, he unexpectedly sang an a cappella version of *Amazing Grace*. I have never heard anything as beautiful, glorious, powerful, and true. Every syllable resonated with Elvis Presley's faith in and love of God. My body trembled from within, and my heart raced, making me lightheaded. My hands and feet felt numb, and I knew the enormity of God. This was the most spiritual experience of my life.

When he finished the song, he smiled at me, and I managed to declare the truest, most obvious statement. "I love you." I swallowed my tears. "I love your faith, your benevolence, your courage and strength, your patriotism, your love for your parents, daughter, and God, your humility and gratitude, your introspection, and your intelligence. Your virtues outweigh your faults."

"Wow. No one has ever told me why before. I love you, too, Caroline. It's funny how we met just a few hours ago, but yet I feel that I've known you for years. You're easy to talk to, you really listen, and you understand me. It doesn't hurt that you're a very pretty girl," he said and winked.

"You're the most beautiful human I've ever seen. I know genetics play a part, but your physical beauty reflects your soul's beauty. Besides, all angels are beautiful."

"What is it people say? Love is blind. But thank you, Little Bit," he said and kissed my forehead. "Hey are you hungry?" Elvis suddenly asked as he glanced at his watch. "It's almost one, and you haven't eaten in hours." He must have seen my hesitation, for he took my hand and stood up. "Come on. Let's go to the kitchen."

Soon, we stood in the kitchen, while he looked around, not quite knowing what to do. I know he rarely cooked or shopped for groceries. The kitchen was not his domain. I cleared my throat. "I can make us something," I offered. There was no need to wake anyone. "What would you like?"

"Oh, you choose, Little Bit." He pointed out the refrigerator and the pantry. After looking, I asked if an omelet would suffice, and he nodded. We sat at the table and talked as we ate, then he helped me rinse the pan and dishes and place them in the dishwasher.

By this point, the incident had moved beyond surreal to normal. Elvis was a man, and he did do everyday things. Besides, it did feel that we were old friends—comfortable and at ease with one another. I smiled up at him. "I do feel that I've known you forever." To my joy, he sang a few lines from his song of that title. As normal as this felt, I was well aware of the once-in-a-lifetime experience under way. I would remember every detail all of my life.

We returned to the TV room, where I blurted out, "I wish I had my Bible with me so I could ask you to sign it."

"No. It wouldn't be right for me to autograph the Bible," he protested.

"Sure it would. I told you how you're the one who brought me deeper and closer to God and His word. You're the perfect person to autograph my Bible. But I had no way of knowing any of this would happen, and it's at my motel room."

Once more, he picked me up, this time carrying me to the second floor, where he opened the door to his personal office. When he turned on the light, I saw framed family pictures, art, and many books. He sat at his desk, pulled something from a drawer, wrote, and came to me a few minutes later.

He held two books, and offered them to me. I wasn't sure what to do, and looked at him as if to ask. Should I take them? "These are for you, Little Bit. Take them."

I did take them, and saw that the top book was a copy of *The Prophet*. I gasped when I looked at the bottom book—a Bible. I felt tears fill my eyes, but I felt torn. I knew how much he enjoyed giving to people, but I had never sought him with the intention of material gain. "I never-I never wanted anything from you. I just wanted you to know what you did for me." I held the books toward him. He shook his head.

"I know that. But those are yours unless I meet another Caroline Hart." He opened the Bible to the presentation page, which he had filled with our names, the date, and the occasion: *Head-on Collision*. I couldn't help but giggle, which pleased him. He then flipped the page to reveal a personal message: *To Caroline, my Little Bit, Thank you for sharing your truth, the fellowship, and the soul connection. Your Friend, Elvis Presley.* He had autographed a Bible for me!

As tears slid down my cheeks, I looked from the Bible to him and told him, "I will read this every day and treasure it. Thank you."

He smiled, nodded, and told me to turn around. I did, never asking or wondering why. He placed something around my neck, and after moving my hair, clasped it. "There. You are one of my girls," he said.

I looked down and saw one of his famous TLC lightning bolt necklaces—resting on my chest. I spun around, stunned. He gently placed two fingers over my lips before I could say anything.

"It's yours. I give these to girls who are special to me. And you are special to me, Caroline Hart."

I stood on my toes and kissed his cheek. "Thank you. I'll wear it constantly and never take it off." His smile made my heart rejoice; his happiness came from giving, and I had witnessed that first-hand. Sure, he bought things for himself, but he most enjoyed sharing his blessings.

He motioned us to a leather sofa. "So you want to be a social worker?"

I nodded. "More than anything."

"Are you still in college?" I shook my head. "You have a job?"

"No, not yet. I want to get my Master's first. I got my B.S. in Behavioral and Health Sciences from Philadelphia University a couple of weeks ago," I explained. "I haven't decided where I want to go to grad school yet. I better decide soon so I can apply." He asked where I was considering going. "Well, Philadelphia is one, of course, but I really do want to get fresh perspectives. So I got information from Cambridge and Harvard, but when I got here last week, I went to U of M to get some information. I like it there."

"Memphis? You'd like to stay in Memphis?" I nodded. "That would be great. Memphis needs people like you to work with families and children. I've seen a lot since my family came here in 1948."

"U of M has a program in Advanced Practice with Children, Youth, and Families that sounds like what I want. I guess I should apply. My transcript can be sent from Philadelphia. I just need to find a part-time job and an apartment. Looks like I made my decision," I said and smiled. "I'll complete my application this week."

"What about your family?"

"I'll call them. They know I was looking out of state, so they won't be too shocked."

"Do you have any brothers or sisters?" he asked me. I knew about his stillborn twin, Jesse.

"No. My mother's pregnancy with me was difficult, so her doctor advised her against getting pregnant again. My parents would have liked another child, but they're okay was just one."

"I wanted my daughter to have a brother or sister so she wouldn't grow up an only child like me. But so far that hasn't happened. It's all in God's hands, though, so if it's meant to be, it will be," he said with a smile.

"Sometimes God doesn't plan our lives the way we want, but I guess He knows what's best, doesn't he?"

"He sure does." He looked at his watch. "Hey, it's nearly 5:00. Wanna go to the best place on the property to watch the sunrise?"

"That would be awesome." I held my precious books while he carried me downstairs. He still refused to let me take the stairs.

Soon we were in the horse corral, facing east. We stood in the gentle early morning breeze while the sun began to tint the sky. After several minutes, I smiled up at him in delight. "This is gorgeous, just like a Monet painting," I exclaimed. "How could anyone deny that God created this world?"

"I don't know, Little Bit. All ya gotta do is look around. Nothing is an accident, nothing. Everything is so perfectly made and formed. This was no cosmic accident billions of years ago. God created the heavens and the earth, and man and woman, and all of the animals and plants, in six days. Six days. That blows my mind, really. Six days. Only God could do all of this."

The wonder and awe in his voice touched my heart deeply. In many ways, he was so much like a little boy, full of curiosity and astonishment. I truly fell in love with the man after spending several hours talking with him.

Before we went in, he took my hand and led me to the horse barn. "I thought you'd like to give Sun his morning treat," he said and pointed to a container of sugar cubes.

I picked up a few and approached the handsome Palomino. I petted his forehead as he ate the sugar cubes. I had seen his picture. Now I was feeding him.

"He's beautiful," I said as we walked out and headed to the house. "Thank you for everything. This has been the most incredible night of my life."

"This sounds like goodbye."

"No, not yet. It's just, this has been more, much more, than I could have ever dreamed. But I will leave soon. You have other things to do." He usually stayed awake nights and slept during the days, a routine prompted by his touring schedule. I knew he needed sleep.

"Not until Dr. Nick checks you again," he reminded me. A little over an hour later, Dr. Nichopoulos examined me, told me to get a more in-depth exam to make sure, and said I could leave.

When I asked if I could use the phone to call a taxi, Elvis refused and insisted on driving me. I told him at which motel I was staying, and panicked. I looked at Jerry, standing nearby, when Elvis led me to the front door. Shouldn't one of them go as a bodyguard just in case? Jerry sprinted to the car and jumped in the back seat, to my relief.

They escorted me to my room, and I hugged Elvis with one arm as I held the books in the other. He patted my back, kissed my cheek, and told me, "Take care, Little Bit, and let me know how U of M goes."

I promised I would, even though I wondered if I would ever see him again.

§§§§§

On Wednesday, July 11, 1973, I took a bus to Graceland, greeting Uncle Vester at the gates. I told him who I was, and said I had a letter for Elvis. He looked at a clipboard in the guard shack and smiled.

"Sure thing, Miss. Elvis had your name put on the list here. I'll make sure he gets your letter."

I thanked him and left, remembering that first encounter of June 6. To be knocked to the ground by none other than Elvis Presley, and to then spend the night talking with him! It all seemed so incredible—and it was. Would I ever see him again? I wondered as I walked to the bus stop.

Five days later, as I returned to my motel room with a small bag of groceries, Jerry approached me. I greeted him as I unlocked the door, and he followed me in. What could he want? I found out.

"How long will it take you to pack all of your things?"

"Pack? Not very long. I didn't bring very much with me. But why?"

"Let's just hurry," he urged, so as my confused brain wondered what this was about, I quickly packed my clothes in my suitcase. Then I gathered all of my U of M papers and the books Elvis had given me, added them to my suitcase, and picked up the bag of groceries. Jerry placed the suitcase in his car, told me he had already informed the manager I was checking out, and rushed me into his car. What?

My head was spinning, but that was mild compared to what he said next. "Elvis wants to see you. He's waiting."

"Really?" I would see him again! "But why did you bring all of my things?"

"We'll be there soon, and Elvis will explain everything," Jerry answered.

Soon, Jerry turned onto a residential street and pulled in the driveway of a small Tudor-style house. He took my suitcase and told me to come with him. We entered the house, and I had to ask myself whose it was. It was tastefully furnished and quite charming, like a storybook house.

"Is Elvis visiting the people who live here?" I asked Jerry after a few minutes. I remained very confused.

"Yes, I am, Little Bit."

I was stunned to watch him come down the stairs—attired in a stylish black suit. "You."

What? I had no idea what he meant, and I said so. "I don't understand. Whose house is this, and why did you want me here?"

"Because it's yours," Elvis said with that beguiling smile.

I stopped breathing in my shock, not one hundred percent sure I wasn't dreaming.

"Here's the deed to your house, Little Bit," Elvis said to me while he held out some papers. "All signed and official. Do you like it?"

I regained my equilibrium. "Like it? It's gorgeous. But this is too much. You can't. . . ."

"I can, and I did. It's all done and legal. Your name is on the deed. It's yours. So is the Cadillac in the driveway," he added as he held the keys and registration out to me.

Jerry nudged my back to let me know not to protest. "I still say this is too much, and it will take a long time to make this seem real. Thank you doesn't seem adequate, but I do thank you." I kissed his cheek. "More than my words can say. I don't know how to thank you."

"But you just did, darlin'. I do know. How about a tour of your house?"

Elvis guided me through the house, and when we got to the master bedroom I nearly cried. It resembled a fairy-tale princess's room, complete with hand-painted furniture and canopy bed. He was excited to show me the second bedroom, which had been converted to a home office.

"Use this for school work and study, then as a bona fide office once you become a social worker," he explained. I couldn't help but hug him in gratitude. "This is okay? I mean, I didn't want to get you too big a house 'cause of the maintenance. It's not too small, is it?"

"Not at all. It's perfect," I assured him. "Absolutely perfect. I'll never have another house, never."

He smiled, happy that he had made me happy. His kindness meant more to me than any treasures ever would.

"Where's my suitcase?" I suddenly asked. Jerry retrieved it from the living room. I removed the Bible and *The Prophet*, placed them on the desk, and said, "Now everything really is perfect."

§§§§

In the weeks leading up to the start of my U of M studies, I made several trips to Goldsmith's department store for supplies, outfits, and shoes. I also called my parents and surprised them with my news. My stunned mother agreed to send my clothes to my new Memphis address.

Of course both my father and my mother peppered me with questions, so I told them everything that had happened since that initial collision.

"Are you sure that bump on your head hasn't caused delusions?" my father asked me.

"I'm quite sure, Dad. I have the autographed Bible Elvis gave me, and I'm calling from my house. I drive the car anywhere I need to go. I wish you could see it all right now. I'll take lots of pictures and send them to you."

"We believe you, honey," my mother assured me. "It's just that this is so fantastic. I mean, a chance encounter like that. We know why you went there, hoping to see him, and I'm so happy it's become more than that for you. You're sure you're all right?"

"Of course I am. I did see another doctor, and I got a clean bill of health. Now I'm just waiting for classes to start so I can get closer to my career."

"We love you, honey. Come visit us for Thanksgiving," my mother instructed. I promised I would.

Finally, August 27 arrived and I attended my first day of M.S. classes. Several challenges awaited me, but I was excited to face them. It wasn't long before I was settled into my new life and academic career, all of which I relished. I looked forward to helping children in particular, but also all people. Now that I was a resident of Memphis, I wanted to help improve the conditions and circumstances in which many people lived. I wanted to help them to break free of the cycles, in which they were trapped, and to become independent. I knew how fortunate and blessed I had been, and I wanted that for all people.

I had been called a dreamer far too often, but there is nothing wrong in dreaming of a better world where people are not burdened by poverty, unemployment, and violence. I longed to be part of the solution, not part of the problem. I truly desired to emulate Dr. John Carpenter.

Elvis was in Las Vegas for a one-month engagement, but on my way home from U of M that first Friday, I stopped at Graceland. I greeted Uncle Vester and handed him a box. He reminded me that his nephew wasn't there.

"I know. This is for you. I hope you like oatmeal cookies."

"I sure do, Miss Caroline. These are for me?" I nodded. He opened the box. "These don't look store-bought. Did you make these for me?"

"Yes, sir. It's just a little token of my appreciation for your kindness."

"Why, thank you," he said and smiled.

I waved, drove home, and thanked God for His blessings.

§§§§§

When my telephone rang on Saturday, September 8, I was surprised to hear Joe on the other end.

"Elvis is renting the Memphian and asked me to invite you. He'd like you to meet his girlfriend Linda and some other people. Can I tell him you'll be here?"

I knew by now not to refuse. Elvis would not have invited me had he not wanted me to go. My emotions felt genuinely moved, and I told Joe this. "Of course I'll be there. Tell Elvis I'm deeply touched."

That evening I drove through the gates of Graceland. How disconcerting to have dozens of people stare into my car windows or take pictures of me and the car. How he ever got used to this I never knew.

Charlie opened the door and pointed me toward the living room. All of the so-called Memphis Mafia milled around, talking, laughing, joking. Elvis was surrounded by people, and I saw Linda chatting with someone else. I stood against a wall, not wanting to interrupt or intrude.

Instead, I looked at the decor more closely than I had done that first evening. I found the family photos most touching, and I walked over to a photograph of Gladys Presley, Elvis's mother. Her smile seemed honest, sincere, and welcoming.

"I wish I had known Mrs. Presley," a woman beside me said.

I looked at her, surprised to see Linda Thompson. I had seen her in pictures with Elvis, so I knew about her. "So do I, Miss Thompson."

"Linda. None of that Miss Thompson business. I'm not a schoolteacher," she told me with a gorgeous smile. "And you must be Caroline. Elvis has told me about you. That was some first meeting you had."

I blushed, but smiled when she giggled. Soon we were talking about college. She had attended Memphis State University, and was even Miss Memphis State University a few years earlier.

"Elvis says you're going to U of M in the social work program. So you want to become a social worker in Memphis?"

I told her about my courses, and she seemed genuinely interested. She was just four years older than I, and had been dating Elvis for thirteen months. Linda was very pretty, but she was also intelligent. She was able to talk with Elvis about spiritual and philosophical topics, which I knew he craved.

"I see you two have met, Mommy and Little Bit," Elvis said with a smile and put one arm around each of us. He gave pet names to the women in his life. "I want my girls to get along. You are the two smartest people I know. I'm gonna end up having to go to college just to talk to you both," he joked.

Within minutes, everyone piled into Lincolns. I was ushered to the car Elvis drove, and boy, was that an experience. It was after midnight, with only streetlights illuminating the streets. Elvis drove very fast, even running a red light, and pulled up at the theater in what seemed like mere seconds.

To my surprise, fans waited outside the theater, and took pictures as we got out of the cars and walked into the theater. How had they known he would be here? The more time I spent with Elvis, the better I understood why he lived as he did. His every act became public knowledge it seemed. I would not want to live with that kind of intense scrutiny.

When I stopped at the fifth row of seats, Linda linked her arm through mine and led me to the front row, where we sat on either side of Elvis. He raised his arm in signal, the lights dimmed, and soon the film began. *The Longest Yard* didn't surprise me, for Elvis's enjoyment of football was well-known. I liked the film, but more than that, I relished seeing him so relaxed, enthusiastic, and into the film.

After approximately half an hour, Elvis motioned to Lamar and Charlie, whispered to them, and they left. Soon they returned with sacks and drinks from Krystal. Everyone was given burgers, fries, and drink. Just over two months after that accidental meeting, I was, at least this night, part of Elvis Presley's inner circle.

§§§§§

I quickly turned on the bedside lamp and grabbed the telephone handset. There was only one person who would call me at 2:10 in the morning. "Elvis, what's wrong?"

"I just want ask you to do something for me, Little Bit."

"Anything. Just tell me what," I said as my heart pounded frantically.

"You know I have to fly to California tomorrow for a few days, right? My divorce is finalized, and we have to appear in court. I never wanted this, not ever. I never imagined this would happen. I wanted Lisa to grow up in a loving family like I did."

"I know, but she will still have a loving family. She knows you and her mother love her very much, and she has her grandparents, aunts, uncles, and cousins who love her. That will never change. You know that."

"Yeah, I do, but it's just not the same as when mommy and daddy are together. It's just not. I don't like that she'll be split between us, traveling back and forth between California and Tennessee. It's not fair to her."

"I know. But I know the two of you will remain friends and do what's best for Lisa. You'll both shower her with love, as always, so in many ways nothing will change. I went to elementary school with a girl whose parents got divorced. The whole thing was nasty and hateful, and her parents loathed each other. My friend's life was miserable, because each parent tried to brainwash her and turn her against the other parent. Nothing like that will happen with you, Priscilla, and Lisa."

"No. But it will never be the same."

"No, it won't, but you will always be her father. If she's even remotely like I am, she'll agree with me that the first and greatest man a girl loves is her daddy. And she is his princess. That never changes, no matter what."

He was silent for several minutes. "No, it won't. Pray for us, Little Bit. Pray for my strength to get through this and to go on living, 'cause right now I sure don't feel like it."

My heart hurt worse than it ever had, but I swallowed my pain for his sake. "I will, Elvis. This can't be easy, but just turn it over to God, and He will get you through this. He will. He knows your pain, and He is here for you. So am I, anytime. I don't care what time it is, call me if there's anything at all I can do. You know how much I love you."

"I do. I don't deserve all of this love, but I sure am grateful for it. I love you, too, Caroline."

He only used my real name when he was in a deep or serious mood. I could hear his pain, and it wounded me. I prayed for his pain to end. We said our goodbyes, hung up, and both of us cried. I could tell he had held his tears back just as I had.

Three days later, I saw the most bittersweet image of all on the evening news. Elvis and Priscilla walked out of the Santa Monica Courthouse arm-in-arm, now ex-spouses. He looked tired, and I knew he was. He was broken-hearted. Both of them were, even through they remained friends and loved one another.

I prayed as a tear slid down my cheek. "Dear God, please watch over Elvis and take care of him. Protect him. This world is too much for him and his sensitive soul. Thank you, God. Amen."

§§§§§

The following Monday, as I walked toward one of my classes, I overheard people excitedly talking. I stopped, listened, and felt fear shoot from the soles of my feet to my heart. "I heard Elvis was just admitted to the hospital." People asked why, but no one knew. One girl called her mother, a nurse at Baptist Memorial, and hung up with a shrug. She told her friends, "She said there's no one there by that name."

Of course not. He always used another name when flying, checking in at hotels, and at hospitals. I knew the pseudonym, but I also knew that hospital staff would not tell me anything. I pondered what to do. The chances of getting in to see him were slim. I could call one of the guys, but I didn't want to add to their stress. I could stand vigil outside the hospital, but what good would that do?

As I debated what to do, I prayed for God's advice. I then knew what Elvis would expect me to do. As much as I longed to know what was wrong with him, I knew I would find out. So I took a deep breath and went into my class. The one-hour class seemed to last one week, but I listened, took notes, and asked questions. I did the best I could, given my intense fear.

As soon as class ended, I ran to my car and drove to Graceland. People were gathered, the news having spread, and I felt my heart pounding hard. People pressed against the locked gate, begging Vester for information. He kept telling them he had none, but that did not stop the requests. I understood that Elvis's fans were concerned; I was, too, of course.

I also understood that, even if Vester knew anything, he would not reveal personal information. I decided to refrain from asking and to keep praying, when Vester noticed me.

"Miss Caroline," he called to me. When I looked up, he motioned me inside the gates. In the guard shack, out of public earshot, we were able to talk. "You heard, too?" I nodded. "We never know how things like this get out, but they do."

I couldn't say anything all of a sudden. My fear was too intense. Vester seemed to notice, and told me, "Don't be scared. We don't know anything yet. Just pray."

I nodded. "I am, constantly. I saw the news footage after the divorce. I was so worried about him. He looked so tired, and I felt he wasn't well. I have been scared, and then people were talking about him being hospitalized. I thought of coming here, I didn't think it was my place or business. But I just had to know if it's true, so I came as soon as class was over."

I tried not to, but I started crying. I turned and left the guard shack, but Vester took my arm and guided me to a nearby golf cart. Before I realized what he was doing, he drove to the house and led me to the door. Jerry answered, surprised to see Elvis's uncle with me, still crying.

"Miss Caroline heard, and she's scared and upset," Vester explained. "Elvis told me to make sure she was taken care of. I don't think she should be driving this upset and crying."

Jerry looked behind him, not seeing anyone, and motioned me in. I protested, saying I would drive home, but Vester remained firm. "No you won't. I'm not gonna be responsible if you have an accident and have Elvis after me. You can drive when you're calm." With that, Vester sped back to his post, leaving me awkwardly in the doorway.

Jerry ushered me in and asked if I'd been at school all day. I nodded. "That's where I heard people saying Elvis had been admitted to the hospital. I almost came here then, but I didn't want to be in the way and be nosy. So I finished class and came after. I just had to know if he's really there. I've been so worried all afternoon. And now I am in the way and butting in where I don't belong. He wouldn't like that. I'm sorry for this. I'll go home and pray for him." I opened the front door, but Jerry pushed it shut.

"He'd hate that we let you go when you're this upset. He understands that the fans want to know because they're concerned. Don't apologize for that. He doesn't want that." I nodded. "Have you had lunch?" he asked me.

I hadn't even thought about food, and shook my head. "I can't eat."

"You have to take care of yourself. Come on, how about a bacon cheeseburger?" Jerry led me to the kitchen, where Pauline Nicholson fixed the burger just the way she did for Elvis, and we sat at the table. "Elvis likes you. He said your faith is strong and you have the kind of values his mother taught him. He likes that you care about people and want to help them."

I held the burger mid-air and stared at Jerry. "He told you that? Did he also tell you he's the biggest influence on me? That he led me to a stronger relationship with God?" Jerry told me no, so I explained all I had told Elvis that first night. "This world really is too much for him. It sucks him dry, drains him. I live with constant fear for him, and so when I heard the other students talking earlier, my fear went into full force. I know God's in charge, but that doesn't mean I'm not afraid and worried."

"We all are. Until they give him the all-clear and release him, we'll be very worried."

After an hour, I assured Jerry I was calmer and capable of driving home. I wanted to walk down the winding driveway and relish the serenity and beauty of the estate. Vester made me promise to get a good night's sleep, and I kissed his cheek before I walked to my car.

The days stretched on with no news, and my worry never dissipated. I prayed frequently, asking God to heal Elvis, to make him well. Despite my fears, I never skipped a class or went to Graceland or the hospital. If I did, I would only be a bother.

My sleep on those nights was restless, so when the phone rang very early on Saturday, October 27, I quickly grabbed the handset. "What's wrong?" I instantly asked.

"Nothing's wrong, Caroline," Linda said in her pretty Southern drawl. "Elvis asked me to call you."

"He did? I've been so worried."

"I'm sure. We all were at first. But he wants to know if you can visit him today."

"Of course I can," I answered, dumbfounded by the request. "What time should I come?"

"Now if you can," Linda said as if it was normal to visit hospital patients at 1:47 A.M.

"I'll be there as soon as I shower and dress."

Forty minutes later, I entered Baptist Memorial Hospital and made my way to the room number Linda had given me. A policeman outside the room asked to see my photo identification, and then opened the door for me.

I was stunned at the sight. Elvis sat cross-legged on the hospital bed, wearing blue pajamas and a silk robe. Linda sat beside him.

"Hey, Little Bit! Come here," Elvis greeted me with a smile. He patted the bed, an indication he wanted me to join them. "How have you been?"

Me? He was the one in the hospital. "Fine, just worried about you."

"I'll be out of here in a week or two. Pneumonia and pleurisy got me. I wasn't feeling well before I went to California. Plus, I've just felt down, you know, like I didn't have any energy. And my stomach's been giving me fits. I thought it was my stomach. Enlarged colon. And hepatitis, so they've been treating all these things. I'm actually better, but they won't let me leave yet. So here we are," he said and smiled at Linda.

He had been extremely sick, just as I had feared. "You're going to be all right?"

"As well as I can be," he said and winked at me.

"That's what I've been praying for," I said, trying to keep the fear out of my voice and eyes. I didn't want to upset him.

"Well, God ain't ready for me yet, Little Bit. He's letting me hang around a little longer."

A little longer? What did he mean by that? Was it just a joke, or did he know something? He was only 38 and had always been energetic. I worried about my mother and Elvis; both of them suffered so, and both tried to brush away the seriousness.

Sure, doctors were treating him, just as doctors tried to treat my mother. But what the doctors did for her never cured her, never took away her pain. I prayed that, since they knew Elvis's ailments, they would, indeed, treat him.

I left the hospital only slightly relieved. Something inside me held onto the fear despite all he and Linda had said. I couldn't explain why, even to myself, but I resolved to overcome fear with faith and prayer. I believed that everything happens for a reason and that often only God knew the reason. I had to trust God.

SSSSS

After classes on Tuesday, November 20, I drove to Graceland. There, I gave Vester a homemade pumpkin pie as well as a gift and card for Elvis. I found a book about Job's steadfast faith throughout his tribulations, and it had helped me. I felt certain Elvis would find it useful, too.

That evening, I took a plane to Philadelphia to spend Thanksgiving with my parents. I would stay until after church on Sunday, then fly back to Memphis. More than anything, I longed to know how my mother felt. I couldn't bear to see her suffering, knowing nothing had helped her.

However, I received a major shock when my parents greeted me at the airport. My mother jumped for joy, ran to me, and embraced me in a very exuberant hug. This was not the same frail woman I had last seen in June.

My father patiently waited while Mom shrieked, kissed me several times, and cried. "She hasn't risen from the dead, Norma. She just came home for Thanksgiving," Dad told her.

"Oh, I know," Mom answered as she placed her hands on my cheeks. "But look at her. Our little girl is a woman now, so grown up and. . . ." Mom held me at arms length and looked me up and down. "Stylish. Where did you get that outfit?"

I giggled. "Linda Thompson and I went shopping in her favorite boutique. I got a few outfits."

"His girlfriend?" I nodded. "You go shopping with Elvis Presley's girlfriend? I'd say you more than met him, Caroline. You're not doing anything immoral are you? You know what they say about rock stars."

"Immoral? Our daughter? Norma, you read too many magazines. Shopping for clothes is far from immoral," Dad reprimanded Mom.

"Oh, I know. But all of those people around him. One never knows."

"Mom, his friends are very nice to me. Elvis treats me like a kid sister. We talk a lot, mostly about life and the Bible."

"Very immoral," Dad said drolly and rolled his eyes.

Mom huffed, I giggled, and we went home. That evening, as I helped Mom prepare dinner, my heart lurched when she said, "Honey, I need to talk to you. Not about you. About me."

She seemed better, but was she worse? "Yes?" was all I could muster.

"I saw the doctors in September, the two I've been seeing for a while. They never were able to find out what was wrong with me. You know that. But, well, in the past few months I just started to feel. . .different. My constant pain got less and less. I was able to sleep more and do more things like before. I wasn't sure what was going on, so I made the appointments just to get examined and make sure something else wasn't going on.

"Both of them thoroughly examined me, did blood and urine tests, took scans of my brain, and x-rays of my lungs. Everything came back negative. They can't explain why, mostly because they don't know what caused the pain in the first place.

"I'm healed, Caroline," Mom said and smiled. "I'm healed."

I stood staring at her for a moment, and then whispered, "It worked."

"What worked? I never did anything differently."

I shook my head. "His prayer for you. God heard him and answered his prayer. It's a miracle, Mom!" I grabbed her in a hug as I cried in joy.

"Who's prayer? What are you talking about?"

"Elvis's." I dried my eyes and told her about his prayer that first night. "Elvis's prayer worked, Mom. He's very special, very spiritual and connected to Heaven. I have to call him and tell him!"

Mom grabbed me before I ran from the kitchen. "Whoa! Slow down. What do you mean Elvis prayed for me? You told him about me? Why?"

"Because he has lots of health issues, and he feels things wrong with him that his doctors can't diagnose. So he did what you did. He found doctors who could help him manage his symptoms. Like you, he just needed to function. I told him I understand what he's going through because my mother was going through something similar. So he took my hands and prayed to God to heal you. And God did!"

"The first night? Didn't this get a bit too personal too soon?"

"No, Mom. We talked about Heaven, his purpose, the Bible. In talking about Elvis's situation, I mentioned what you did, because he did the same thing. That's all. If both of you sought medications to help you, how many other people have done the same?"

"But he doesn't know me," Mom said, still grasping what I'd told her.

"That doesn't matter. He loves God, and he loves people. He's a Christian. Christians pray for one another, don't they?"

"Oh, yes, I suppose. But you do realize it's not every day that my daughter tells me Elvis Presley prayed for me. That's not the usual experience."

"I know, Mom, but that's who he is. Prayer is part of his daily life. I do want to call him."

"Isn't it too early? I mean, it's 5:30. Isn't he a night owl?"

I hadn't considered the time. "Yes, he is. I'll call after midnight."

"You're not staying up all night all the time, are you? What about college?"

"No, Mom. Sometimes on Saturday nights, I go to the movies with them, things like that. But he wouldn't ask me to stay up on a school night. He really is quite protective of me, like a big brother."

"My surrogate son, the King of Rock 'n Roll. Of course, I've never mentioned your knowing him to anyone."

"It's okay, Mom. I've been caught in some pictures since June, but I think most of those have been in Memphis newspapers. I don't think they know who I am, though. I just happen to be there. It's certainly not me they're after."

"I hope not. You don't need that, not with school."

During dinner, Mom told Dad about Elvis's prayer, and, in his shock, he dropped his fork. I had to repeat the story for him, and he was less dazed by what transpired that first night than Mom had been.

"See, Norma, real immoral stuff," he teased her.

We all had a good laugh, and I helped Mom clean up. We watched television for a while, until Mom and Dad went to bed. I sat in the living room, clutching a sofa pillow to me, while I pondered all that had happened to me since June 6. Five months, nearly 6 months.

I had done more than meet the man who had led me toward my salvation. I'd come to know him first-hand. He was just as I had known he was: spiritual, benevolent, mischievous, humble but aware of his gifts, complex, needy, temperamental, and often lonely, even in a crowd. Most of all, he was a searcher. He sought his life's true purpose. And he sought what, or rather who, he had lost—his mother. He was a man-child, and he craved a maternal figure. Linda was that for him; one of his pet names for her was Mommy.

As much as he gave to the world, he needed the security, protection, and love that only his mother had provided. Gladys had also defined his life's reason. Everything he had done was motivated by his desire to take care of her. They had not lived in Graceland one year before Elvis was drafted. Her health already tenuous, the separation from her only surviving child led to her decline. I believed that. I also felt that he sustained guilt over her death. If he had not left home, he could have helped her, he could have done something. This was, I knew, his heaviest burden, and only their reunion in Heaven would end it.

I wiped tears from the corners of my eyes, and then smiled. Elvis was also a superhero. His dyed black hair, the sideburns, the jumpsuits and capes, lightning bolt symbol (Taking Care of Business in a Flash) all pointed to his favorite childhood comic book. Young Freddie Freeman was given powers and transformed into Captain Marvel, Jr.

Elvis was given gifts and abilities. He transformed himself to Marvel, Jr.'s clone. He also used his karate skills to thwart would-be villains in real-life situations. He openly acknowledged his dream of being a comic book hero in his 1970 Jaycee's speech. He really was a superhero. He was my superhero.

After hours of thinking, I looked at the clock. 12:43. He should be awake by now. I dialed his direct number, to his private phone in his bedroom, and he answered immediately.

"Yeah?" was all he said.

"Am I disturbing you? It's Caroline."

"Hey, Little Bit, I thought you went to your parents'."

"I did. I'm here now. But I had to call you. I have the most wonderful news."

I told him what my mother had revealed to me, and gushed, "You saved her!"

"Whoa, whoa, whoa. Slow down. I didn't heal her. I just prayed for her. God healed her, Little Bit. I knew He would."

"Because of you, He did. It took your prayer, Elvis. Yours. Lots of people have prayed for Mom, but it took your prayer. She said she started feeling better over the past few months. We met five months ago. It's your prayer, your strong faith, that got God's attention. I know it."

"So her pain is gone?" he asked, diverting the topic.

"Yes. How are you?" He paused for a few seconds, just long enough to alarm me.

"I'm doing well, as well as can be expected."

"Has your pain been worse since we met?"

"What? Why would it?"

"Remember what I told you about empaths? Some empaths subsume the energies and physical ailments of others. My mother's pain suddenly disappeared, and you got sick. I just wonder if you didn't take her pain into your body."

He was quiet far too long for my ease. "I want to do some reading on this empath business," he finally said. "How do you know so much about this? You're one, too, aren't you?"

"Yes. That's one reason I picked up what was going on with you. But I never had an impact on my mother. I'm not as advanced as you are," I explained.

"I never heard of this until you mentioned it," he said. "I never knew all of this is a thing. Maybe all of this explains the headaches and insomnia," he mused.

"I'm sure it does. That's why it's so important that you take care of yourself. Please."

"Don't you worry about me, Little Bit," he said before we said goodbye.

Of course I was worried about him. I would always worry about him. He took on too much from the world, and he didn't take care of himself. He placed others' needs ahead of his own, and as a result, his own health suffered.

I finally went to bed in my old room, but didn't sleep. Instead, I clutched my childhood teddy bear close to me and stared up at the ceiling. "Dear God, please watch over Elvis and take care of him. He's a giver, not a taker, you know that, and he puts his own health last. Open his eyes and mind to the importance of caring for himself. He doesn't sleep right, eat right, get enough sunlight. I'm scared for him, God. He's working too much. He's working himself to death. I know you have more for him to do on earth, but he needs to stay healthy enough to do everything destined for him. Please, God, I ask you to end his suffering. Amen."

I prayed for Elvis every day, every night and morning, during my father's Thanksgiving supper prayer, during Sunday morning church services. When the choir sang *In the Garden*, all I could hear was Elvis's magnificent voice.

As much as I enjoyed being with my parents, I was anxious to return to Memphis. I knew I couldn't and wouldn't spend time with Elvis, and I did have classes the following day, but I just longed to be physically closer to him. My parents noticed my restlessness as we waited at the airport.

"What is so urgent that you can't wait to get out of here?" my mother asked.

"Does it show? I didn't mean for it to. I enjoyed coming home and being with both of you. Really. But. . . ." I struggled to say the truth. I didn't want to hurt my parents.

"But your life is in Memphis now. Right?" My father always read me well. I nodded, tears forming in my eyes. "No need for tears. You went there for what was supposed to be a short vacation. I recall you telling me you doubted you'd ever get near this idol of yours, but you hoped you would. Well, fate intervened, and you did more than that. Your idol is now your friend. That's pretty amazing. Not many people can say that. But there's something else, isn't there, Caroline?"

My heart pounded. I dared not ask what he meant. I stared at my shoes, avoiding his eyes. However, his hand on my chin forced my head up, and I looked at my father.

"You love him."

"Of course I do. He's an incredible human being, so. . . ."

"No," Dad interrupted me. "You love him." He stared at me until his meaning penetrated my skull.

"But he has a girlfriend. Linda is so nice, and she's good for him."

"That may be true, but it doesn't stop your feelings. Nothing can. He'd be an idiot not to see it. Just guard your heart. Don't let him break it."

"Him? Break my heart? He couldn't."

"What if he remarries?"

"Then I'll be happy for him. He deserves love and happiness. Yes, I love him. That's not a secret, even from him. I've told him several times."

"Uh-huh. Okay, I believe you," Dad said and changed the subject. We chatted for a few minutes.

I hugged and kissed him and Mom, boarded the plane, and stared at the clouds.

"What was all of that about?" Mom asked Dad after I left them. "You really think she's going to get hurt?"

"Sure, I do." He then answered Mom's unasked question. "He's not well. He's been in the hospital a few times lately. I'm not worried about his girlfriends. I'm worried about him doing the worst thing that can happen to Caroline. Dying."

"Harvey! Don't even think such a thing!"

"Well, you heard her. You know what was wrong a couple of weeks ago. If he dies, what will it do to Caroline? That's what scares me."

§§§§§

The rest of 1973 remained peaceful and uneventful—thankfully. I completed my first semester of grad school successfully, making the Dean's List. I had five weeks off before the spring semester began.

I bought Christmas gifts for my parents, Uncle Vester, Linda, and Elvis. I was not privy to Elvis's holiday plans, but

I knew I could leave his and Linda's gifts with Vester if I didn't see them.

My parents wanted me to come home, but I really longed to spend my first independent Christmas at my Memphis home. They understood, and I had their presents shipped to them.

However, I would not get to spend Christmas at my home. My phone rang on Saturday, three days before Christmas. Linda answered my salutation.

"Hi, Caroline. I know it's late notice, and you probably have plans, but Elvis asked me to call you. He'd like you to come over on Christmas and spend the day with us. Can you?"

To say I was stunned was definitely an understatement. More than that, my heart was touched. I fought my tears as I responded. "I'd love to. Thank you, and tell Elvis I'm honored."

"I will. See you in a few days."

I looked at their wrapped presents under my tree, glad I hadn't yet taken them to Uncle Vester. On Saturday, I placed them in my car and drove through Graceland's gates. The Nativity scene on the front lawn made me smile. Christmas was, most of all, a commemoration and celebration of Jesus's birth. Gift giving carried on the tradition begun by the Three Wise Men. That's how I defined Christmas, and Elvis, I knew, felt similarly.

Linda welcomed me at the door, took my coat, and led me to the den, which was gleaming with Christmas lights that gave the room a sunset glow. Elvis, his father and step-mother, and his grandmother sat on chairs and sofas. Elvis leapt from his chair when he saw us.

He hugged me, and said, "I'm so glad you came, Little Bit." He introduced me to his family, told me to put the gifts under the tree, and ordered me an orange juice from the kitchen.

We all chatted for more than an hour before dinner was announced. The elegant dining room contained another tree. I could see how much Elvis enjoyed celebrating Christmas. I doubted his family had ever had a tree in Tupelo, but I did know that they understood the true significance of the holiday. Riches were important to Elvis primarily because his wealth enabled him to provide for his family and to give to others. He truly exemplified Christ.

Elvis caught me looking at him as I thought, and he winked and nodded at me. Once again, he seemed to know what I was thinking. I smiled at him, recognizing how blessed I was to know him.

I delighted in watching Elvis interact with his grandmother, whom he fondly called Dodger. They loved each other deeply. I spent more time observing and taking in every detail than I spent eating.

After dinner, we all returned to the den. Elvis gave his family members their gifts from him, and handed Linda two large boxes. To my utter surprise, he gave me a present. Next, Vernon gave his wife, mother, son, and Linda their gifts from him. Tentatively, I went for my gifts for Elvis and Linda, which I gave to them. I smiled as I listened to their joking, chattering, and laughter as they began to open their gifts. I caught Linda's eye, and she motioned for me to open my present from Elvis.

I very carefully removed the ribbon, unfolded the paper, and was not surprised to see a book. I had noticed the title on a shelf in his upstairs office. This was a 1942 first edition of Albert Camus's *The Stranger*, the story of a man who is condemned not for the crimes he commits, but because he reacts differently to life events than most people do. Elvis had inscribed the book to me with the date "*Christmas 1973.*"

I smiled, thinking how similar our gifts to each other were. When he finally opened his from me, he looked it over and beamed at me. I hadn't inscribed the book but I had tucked a note to him inside, which he read silently:

Dear Elvis,

Thank you for being my white knight and superhero. You are among the greatest of men ever created by God.

Thank you for sharing yourself and your gifts with the world. Thank you for showing me the way.

With all of my love and gratitude.

XOXO,

Caroline

He leapt from his chair and pulled me into a hug.

"Thank you for the Camus novel. I will read it over winter break," I said.

"We'll talk about it after you do. We also need to talk about this one," he said and held up the book I had given him. "The title has me curious and interested. *Being and Nothingness.* You've read it?"

I nodded. "I'm sure it will make you think. It's an essay in which Sartre claims that one's existence precedes one's essence and that we all have free will. It really helped me to solidify my Christian beliefs, because Sartre claims that who we are is not pre-determined. We create ourselves."

"So it will challenge our beliefs?"

"Yes, but I know yours are as strong as or stronger than mine. Yours won't bend or break. We know God is in control."

"Yes, we do, Little Bit. Yes, we do."

SSSSS

The next few months passed without major incidents. However, my excitement mounted went Elvis's March 1974 concerts were announced. Five concerts in Memphis! I knew I had to be first in line to buy tickets to all five. I had never seen Elvis perform except on television and in films, and attending an Elvis concert was a long-held dream.

The tickets went on sale on a school day, but if I staked my place in line the night before, I could buy my tickets early and not miss class. On my way to the venue the night before, someone honked at me while I sat at a traffic light. I glanced over. Dr. Nichopoulos.

I rolled down my window, and he asked where I was going.

I smiled and gushed, "To stand in line for the concert tickets!"

"All night?"

"Of course. I want good seats."

He smiled and went his way, but shocked me by coming to the coliseum over an hour later.

"You don't need to stand here any longer. Let's go," he said.

I'm sure I looked horrified. "But I need my tickets. I can't leave."

Other people also stood in line, one in front of me and several behind me. "You plan to attend all five shows?" I nodded. "Fine. Come with me. Trust me, Caroline."

I could tell he didn't want to say too much in front of everyone, but I couldn't leave. Tears filled my eyes.

Dr. Nichopoulos leaned close and whispered in my ear. "You're going. It's all arranged."

"How?" I asked

"Let's go, and I'll tell you."

At my car, he said he had called Joe and had me put on the guest list. I would sit in the front row with Elvis's family and friends.

I hugged him and kissed his cheek. "You didn't have to do that. But thank you! I'm going to donate the money I'd have spent on the tickets to one of Elvis's charities."

"He'll like that. Now go home."

Finally March 16 arrived, and I drove to Mid-South Coliseum, where Dr. Nichopoulos arranged to meet me backstage. Elvis was scheduled to perform two shows that day and the following day, and one show a few days later, on the 20th—his last of that tour.

Elvis, Linda, his father, and his entourage arrived, and he greeted Dr. Nick and me, kissing me on the cheek. We could feel the electricity in the building as people eagerly awaited the hometown hero. We couldn't really hear anything distinctly, but Joe informed Elvis that he had fifteen minutes before the *2001* theme.

Joe quickly escorted Dr. Nick, Linda, Mr. Presley, and me to our seats, where we joined Linda's parents and Mrs. Parker. Other friends of Elvis's were in the front row, and I was quickly introduced to them.

"You look pretty," Linda said with a smile. "Is that a new dress?" I nodded, as nervous and excited as I had ever been. Sure, I had met him, but seeing Elvis perform would be a new and thrilling experience—and not once but five times!

"I understand. He's your idol, and this is your first concert, isn't it?"

"Yes. I yearned for this chance so long. The closest I came was watching *Aloha from Hawaii* earlier this year. This isn't a dream, I know that, but it's my dream come true."

Linda gave me a hug just as the lights dimmed and the *2001* theme began. Excitement mounted, erupting after the theme, when the TCB band played the opening riff. Elvis bounded on stage, resplendent, the studs on his jumpsuit sparkling like the diamonds on his fingers.

Tears fell from my eyes, and I stared at Elvis as he walked across the stage waving at fans. He stopped in front of us and smiled down at me. My heart overflowed with love, gratitude, and happiness.

Fans screamed, clapped, vibrated the coliseum. As the show progressed, Elvis threw scarves to women in the front rows. Security lined the front of the stage, preventing anyone access to Elvis, but that didn't dampen the enthusiasm.

Elvis looked and sounded incredible, and he truly enjoyed himself. I thanked God, for Elvis deserved this. He felt the love of the audience, and it showed.

After he was rushed off stage, he was driven back to Graceland to rest before the evening show. I was invited to the mansion, as well, and at first declined, saying I didn't want to interfere or exhaust him.

I shouldn't have worried. He was in his suite, away from the crowd for a while. Linda went up, of course, and when they came down, he had changed into another jumpsuit. He chatted with his friends, and then came to me.

"Linda told me this was your first concert."

"Yes. I don't know how to tell you how magnificent you were." Tears filled my eyes again. "Thank you."

"Thank you, Little Bit. That means everything to me. You'll be there tonight, too, right?" I nodded. "Good. I'll look for you."

Soon, we all left for the coliseum again, and as before, we all sat close to the front. Even though it had only been a few hours since the previous concert, I was equally mesmerized and spellbound. Many of the songs were the same, but Elvis never sang a song exactly the same twice. Each performance was unique and different. He took my breath. He filled my soul.

When Elvis began loosening the white scarf from his neck, women began reaching, pleading, and screaming. Security must have been alerted, for one of the officers reached for my hand and led me to the front of the stage. I have no idea how my body moved, because I felt numb.

Elvis knelt and placed the scarf around my neck, kissed my cheek, and smiled at me. I returned the kiss and told him, "I love you."

"For my good friend, Caroline," he said into the microphone and continued singing. As I turned, camera flashes exploded, and I was momentarily blinded. I was helped into my seat, where Dr. Nichopoulos and Mr. Thompson made sure no one stole my scarf. No one even tried, thankfully.

The day was magical, and I didn't sleep that night. I placed the scarf in a small chest my mother had given me, and I locked it securely. How had my life gonc from dreams to living a reality beyond any of my dreams? In less than one year, I had not only seen and met Elvis Presley, but was his friend. "Thank you, God," I said as I stared at the ceiling.

Monday morning on campus, my classmates were abuzz about my moment in the spotlight. Most had attended the concert and had seen Elvis give me the scarf. All had seen my picture in Sunday morning's newspaper. I smiled and said that his act had surprised me, but I refused to say more. I was even asked by a few people to autograph the picture—but why I couldn't grasp.

The two Sunday shows and the Wednesday show were stupendous, and Elvis sold out all five concerts. No one was surprised by that. I was so amazed by him. I saw how much energy he expended at each concert and how that exhausted him. My love and respect for him increased each day. I went to bed that night elated but concerned. As always, I prayed to God for Elvis's health and well-being.

§§§§

With my graduation in December, my coursework increased with my Master's dissertation. I conducted field research as I job shadowed social workers, which was essentially a full-time job.

I occasionally saw Elvis, but with our schedules, not as frequently as I would have preferred. However, I received a telephone call from Joe in mid-September asking if I wanted to attend a filming at the Tennessee Karate Institute on the 16th. Elvis would talk about and demonstrate karate.

"I'd love to. I hate to ask, but a little boy I've been working with adores Elvis. He doesn't have a father figure, and I know this would thrill him. May I bring him? His name is Marcus, and he's ten years old."

"Sure. Elvis love kids. I'll add you both to the list."

"Am I really gonna see Elvis?" Marcus asked me when I shared the news.

"Of course. You'll see him demonstrate karate and hear him talk about it, too. I'm very excited, too, Marcus. I know what this means to you."

He nodded. "I used to make believe he was my daddy, but he couldn't be around because of all the concerts and stuff. I wish he was my dad. He's so cool."

Tears filled my eyes, and I fought them with every ounce of my strength. "Yes, he is, and he would adore a son like you. He always wanted a son, he told me."

"He does? I hope he has one someday. He's too nice to not get what he wants in life," Marcus said in his ten-year-old wisdom.

I kissed the top of his head and told him, "Yes, he is."

I picked up Marcus on Saturday, and his eyes became large when his mother brought him outside.

"Wow! Is this the Cadillac that Elvis gave you?" I told him it was. "And I get to ride in it? Cool! This is gonna be the best day ever!"

"I know, Marcus. Mrs. Joyner," I said and looked at his mother, "I will take good care of Marcus and keep him with me the entire time. Elvis's bodyguards will be there, so he will be safe."

"I ain't worried 'bout that. Just make sure he's on his best behavior and polite. If he gives you any trouble, you let me know when you bring him home."

"Marcus is a perfect gentleman all the time. I'm positive he will be today, too. I don't know how long this will last. Is that a problem?"

"No. Just thank you for this. It means the world to him."

"My pleasure," I said, and soon Marcus and I were at the Tennessee Karate Institute. "You know, Elvis founded this Institute, Marcus. His friends manage it for him. I've never been here, either, so I'm very excited, too. You ready?"

He nodded enthusiastically, his smile huge, and we entered the building and were shown where to stand. Marcus's growing anticipation warmed my being, but never matched my own. Meeting Elvis, seeing him in concert, and now witnessing him doing one of his greatest passions. My heart raced as we waited.

Then the wait was over, and Linda entered and waved at the camera, looking beautiful as always, followed moments later by some of his entourage. Elvis came in wearing his custom karate gi, white with red and black accents. I inhaled sharply. He appeared happy, in a good mood, and enthusiastic about the film project. His famous handsome looks never failed to melt my heart completely; that day, he looked amazing.

Marcus poked my arm and whispered, "You love him."

"Yes, I do, very much. He means the world to me," I responded.

"I hope you told him that."

"I did, Marcus. I did."

"Good. I hope I get to tell him what he means to me."

"I'll make sure you do," I promised.

After exhilarating demonstrations and lessons and talks by Elvis and other experts, the filming for the day wrapped up. Elvis met and signed autographs for many young karate students and other attendees. Finally, I took Marcus to meet his idol.

"Mr. Elvis, you're the coolest man ever, just like a real-life superhero. I never knew my dad, never had a dad. I told Miss Caroline I wish you were my dad. You're just the best."

Elvis put his hand on Marcus's cheek and said, "Marcus, I'd be proud to have you as my son. Caroline must think you're pretty special to bring you here today. Do you like karate?"

Marcus nodded. "Yes, Sir!"

"I tell you what, how would you like lessons here as long as you like?"

"I'd love it, but Mama can't afford lessons, but thank you."

"She doesn't have to, Marcus. Free lessons, my gift to you," Elvis said.

"Really? Wow! Then I'll be just like you!"

"Do me proud, son. Use karate to protect yourself and others. Will you do that?"

"Yes. Thank you, Mr. Elvis," Marcus said and hugged Elvis.

I smiled at Elvis with tears filling my eyes, and said a silent, *"Thank you, God, for this gift to Marcus and to Elvis."*

§§§§§

My parents arrived in Memphis on Thursday, December 12 in order to attend my Master's graduation on Saturday. For the first time, they saw the Cadillac and the house Elvis had bought me. Both proclaimed the home charming and just right for me.

"I think so, too. I plan to keep the Cadillac forever and never move from this house. They were gifts from the most incredible man, and they mean so much to me. I want to grow old in this house with all of my mementos and memories," I told them.

"Plans change, Caroline. Life has a way of taking us places we never expected to go," my father cautioned me.

"I'm never leaving my home, my first and only home. Not for anything or anyone."

My father dropped the subject. Mom asked, "Will we get to meet Elvis? Is he in Memphis?"

I went to the kitchen to make tea, followed by my parents. "Caroline?"

"No, he's not. He's in Las Vegas." My mother asked if he was performing. I shook my head. "No. He's staying at Dr. Ghanem's home, being treated for a nonpenetrating ulcer crater with edematous mucosal folds. He's undergoing his second sleep diet there." I had memorized what Charlie had told me when he called to say that Elvis wouldn't be back in time for my graduation.

Thankfully, my parents didn't ask further questions. I couldn't have answered them anyway. I did my best to hide my concern around them.

On Saturday morning, my father answered the doorbell and then called me downstairs. "These were just delivered for you."

"For me? Really? Who on earth would send me flowers?"

"I couldn't begin to guess," Dad said wryly. "Open them and see if I'm right."

"Long-stemmed roses! Oh, they're beautiful! I've never gotten roses before!" I removed the card, opened it, and walked to a corner holding it to my chest.

"I was right," my father said and gave the roses to my mother to tend. "Elvis."

I nodded, my throat too choked with tears to speak. Even now, sick and in treatment, he thought of me. "*Dear God,*" I silently prayed, "*please take care of Elvis. Please. Take care of him.*"

That night and many nights afterward, I cried myself to sleep, each night making the same prayer for God to take care of him. My existence revolved around his health and well-being, around his getting well. That was my mantra and my prayer each morning and each night.

§§§§§

My parents called me Christmas morning, which was nice. We chatted for almost two hours, reliving past holiday

99

memories and stories. I spent the rest of the day reading and watching neighborhood children building a snowman on their front lawn, and wondering how Elvis was.

The ringing telephone startled me. Who could it be? I wondered. "Hello?" I asked, curious to know.

"Merry Christmas, Little Bit."

"Elvis! Merry Christmas! I've been thinking about you all day. Oh, it's so good to hear your voice. I was going to drop by the front gates in a little while."

"Well, it's good to hear yours, too. Why are you going to the gates? Just come on up to the house. That's why I'm calling, to see if you want to come over for a while." I paused for a few seconds, enough for him to pick up why. "It's been a while since we've seen each other. I wouldn't have called if I didn't want you here. Come on."

I told him I would, and moments later, the gates opened and I drove up to the house and was let inside. Elvis was in the living room with friends and family, so I went in and joined them, getting more used to doing so.

After talking for a few hours, some people left for home and others drifted off to do their own things. I had a few minutes alone with him, so I took the chance for private Christmas wishes for Elvis.

"It's not much, and it's not grand, but I thought of you when I saw this," I told him and placed a small box in his hand. When shopping in a jewelry store, I'd seen a gold Ten Commandments Bible bookmark that instantly made me think of Elvis.

He opened it and smiled. "This is beautiful. I'll keep it in my Bible to remind me of you," he said and hugged me. "Thank you, honey."

"Anytime I see a Bible or anything to do with the Bible, I just think of you immediately. That's my first thought when I think of you: your faith and belief. And how you helped strengthen my own. That's a gift I can never repay."

"Oh, but you can. You do. Just by being you and having a strong faith, letting people see God in you. That's enough. Then there's your work with people, like Marcus. How is he, by the way?"

I beamed. "He's fine. He really enjoys those karate lessons. When I can, I take him and watch him. He really does think the world of you. So do I. I hope you know that, Elvis."

"I do," he very softly said. "I do."

VERSE TWO:

AN EVENING PRAYER

I drove to Graceland very early on a Wednesday morning in early January 1975. The night guard at the gates let me in, having seen me several times over the past year and a half. I glanced at my watch: 2:45. He should be awake. I hoped so. This was a very special Wednesday, Elvis Presley's 40th birthday.

I was let in, and told that few people had seen Elvis since Christmas, that he had holed himself in his bedroom, allowing few people entrance. However, one of the guys telephoned his private line and told Elvis I was there. A moment later, I was told to go on up.

I had never entered his private room, only his office. Outside the doors,

I took a very deep breath and gently rapped on the door. His very familiar voice beckoned me in, and I turned the doorknob and entered.

He and Linda sat on the bed, and I greeted them both. I walked to him, smiled, and said, "Happy birthday, Elvis!"

"You came all the way over here in the middle of the night just to say that?"

"When else could I say it on the actual day? You'll be asleep when I get out of class this afternoon, so now is my only chance to say happy birthday to you. Besides, it's a chance to see you, which is always very special to me." I looked at him, as he smiled at me, and asked, "How are you?"

"I'm hangin' in there, Little Bit. Just resting up before I hit the road again. How have you been doing?"

"Just fine. Always thinking of you and praying for you, always. You mean the world to me, I've told you that. I mean that."

"Well, you mean a lot to me to, Caroline, an awful lot. Hang on, honey, I've got to make a phone call real quick."

Just a few minutes after he had hung up, his stepbrother arrived with a packet of pills for Elvis. I watched as he took the pills, leaned his head back for a moment, and then smiled at me.

I didn't know what to do or to say. I had known, of course, of his drug use, but I had never before seen him take the drugs. I knew some of them were for self-medication, but not all of them. I understood addiction, and I knew he had an addiction, an addiction that terrified me.

"Here," I said and held a gift and card out to him. "I got this for you, and I know you will enjoy it."

"You didn't have to do that, Little Bit, but thank you." He opened the package, and smiled when he saw Khalil Gibran's *Voice of the Master*. "Come here, honey," he said and held out his arms toward me.

I bent down and hugged him as he wrapped his arms around me, and I took the greatest chance of my life. "Elvis, please take care of yourself. There is only so much God can do. He expects us to do our part. So please, for yourself, for your daughter, for your father and your family, for Linda, for your fans, and for me, stop. Please stop. You have to."

I felt him tense, and I feared my comments would end our friendship. I had angered and hurt him. But I could not live with myself if I had not said something to him. Too many people, for various reasons, refused to say anything, to talk to him about his addiction. I had to. I couldn't let him self-destruct. I couldn't.

"I love you. I may never see you again after this, but I will always love you. Remember that. Goodbye."

I walked toward the door, ready to leave Graceland, perhaps for the last time. "What do you mean goodbye? Come back here."

I held my breath and walked back to his side, expecting a tirade. Instead, he patted the bed beside him, told me to sit, and took my hand.

"Thank you for caring about me, Little Bit. Don't worry about me, I've got it covered. I'm going to kick this habit as soon as the next tour is over, I promise you. So don't worry about me."

"I will always worry about you. That's part of love. That's part of friendship."

He deftly changed the subject, and the three of us chatted for a while longer before I left and returned home. I lay awake, praying to God to take care of him, as I did every night and every day, until it was time to shower and dress for classes.

How could a happy event like a birthday leave me with fear and uncertainty? He was not well, and the sad truth was it was partly his fault. There was nothing Dr. Nichopoulos, Linda, his family and friends, or I could do if he refused to make the first move. Nothing, and I had never felt more defeated and terrified.

§§§§§

That night, and every night for months, I cried myself to sleep. As I cried, I also prayed, prayed for God to end Elvis's suffering, to end his pain— both physical and psychological—and to heal him. I was tortured and terrified, in constant fear of the news I most dreaded.

Exactly three weeks after his 40th birthday, news spread that Elvis had been rushed to Baptist Memorial Hospital. I could only pray for him, that he got the treatments he so desperately needed, and that it wasn't serious health issues as the hospital spokesman told people. I knew by now that Col. Parker kept the drug abuse from the public, so any treatments for that would never be revealed publicly.

My telephone rang a few days later; my father was checking on me. "This is serious isn't it, Caroline? How are you?"

"Me? I'm fine. I'm worried about Elvis, if that's what you mean. Of course I am. Is that so unusual?"

"What's all this about liver problems? What kind of problems?"

What could I say? How could I answer that? That was the hospital's official statement, but even I didn't know if it was true or not. I explained that to my father, and said, "Despite his fame, Elvis is a really private person, Dad. I can't tell you anything specific, because I don't know exactly what's true. I have my instinct, but I can't prove it, so I won't say anything. Just pray for him, please just pray. I'm so scared, Dad, so very scared."

Elvis was hospitalized until mid-February, and I rarely saw him for months. I continued to pray several times daily, and my nights were plagued by dreams and nightmares that starred Elvis and me. In one of them, which frequently recurred, he was trapped in a cell, begging me to free him. I tried with all of my might and resources, but I was never able to release him. No one else was ever around to help me, leaving me on my own, defenseless to save the man I loved.

Despite the constant fear, the lack of sleep, and the uncertainty, my life had to continue. After my graduation, I continued to work part-time at the social work agency, because there were no full-time positions available. I enjoyed the work, the people, the challenges, and most of all that it kept my mind occupied. I also felt grateful that I could help people, even a little bit.

In March, one of the social workers announced that she would retire the first week of April. I was encouraged to apply for her position, and I felt elated when I became a full-time social worker. My first official day on the job was Monday, April 7, 1975.

To my delight, among my first clients was Marcus Joyner. I had developed a connection and a bond with Marcus, and I was pleased that we could continue our relationship. My other clients kept my days full and busy, making it seem as if time sped by at a supersonic speed.

One very bright spot that summer happened on June 10 at Mid-South Coliseum when Elvis performed once more in his hometown. He seemed in good spirits, clowning with the audience, kissing dozens of ladies, and eliciting nonstop screams and adulation. It eased my heart to see him having fun on stage.

I saw him before and after the concert, and even though he looked tired and bloated, he appeared happy and in a good mood. I knew, though, that he continued to take the medications, which troubled my heart and my soul.

Other than that concert, I rarely saw Elvis, although I never stopped praying for him. The restless nights continued, and so did the bad dreams—or, I should say, the prophetic dreams. My fear became so great that I stopped watching or reading the news. I didn't want to hear or to read the words '*Elvis Pressley Died Today.*' I never wanted to hear or see those words.

On August 21, however, I once more plummeted into deepest fear when he was again admitted to Baptist Memorial Hospital. After just three days and five shows at the Las Vegas Hilton, Elvis flew back to Memphis to be admitted to the hospital. The official cause: fatigue.

Yes, he was exhausted, but I also knew that the combination of illness and drug abuse had already taken a tremendous toll on his body. He could not continue to abuse his already ailing body much longer without serious repercussions.

I cried myself to sleep that night, as usual. I don't remember what time I finally went to sleep. I don't remember much, except waking up and screaming, "No!" What had happened? What had awakened me? My heart pounded furiously, and I felt more terrified than I ever had. I clutched the bed sheet tightly as I sat in my dark room for over one hour.

The next several nights were similar, with unremembered nightmares that awakened me and thrust me into the deepest, darkest pits of terror. I never remembered those nightmares, and for that I was grateful, even though I had a pretty good idea what they were about.

On a Saturday morning in September, I once more awoke screaming from a nightmare. I looked at my clock. 3:18. I sat against the headboard, unwilling to succumb to sleep and night terrors once more. I hugged my knees to me and tried to meditate in the darkness to alleviate my fear. Suddenly, the telephone rang, and I jumped.

I grabbed the handset, expecting the worst news, only to hear that voice greet me. "Hey, Little Bit, did I wake you?"

"Elvis. No. I was awake. Are you all right? What's going on?"

"I just wanted to talk to someone. Tell me about your job. What's it like?"

He had been in the hospital for four weeks at this point, and I knew he was restless. He was bored. He was not the sort of man who could stay still and in one place for too long. So I told him about my job, the clients with whom I worked, my co-workers, my schedule, and how much I thoroughly enjoyed every aspect of being a social worker in Memphis.

"I'm sure glad you decided to stay here in Memphis. I really am. It's good to have friends like you, who really care about me and who pray for me. You do still pray for me don't you, Caroline?"

"Of course I do. You never need to ask me that. I will always pray for you, Elvis. Other than my parents, you are the most important person in the world. You are my superhero, my path to freedom, the freedom that matters most, the freedom of knowing God and His purpose for me. So yes, I pray for you several times each day and night, and I always will."

"I know that, Little Bit. Thank you. I just wanted to hear your voice, to talk to you for a little while. I'll see you when I'm out of here, I promise. Okay?"

"I'll like that, Elvis.   And remember, please take care of yourself."

§§§§§

Elvis was released on September 25, although I didn't see him for a month after. I thought of and prayed for him constantly, and continued to have the bad dreams that often awakened me in fear. I tried to convince myself that the dreams resulted from my fevered brain; after all, I still cried myself to sleep each night. I knew they weren't, though, and that they were products of my subconscious mind trying to warn me.

I wrote everything in the diary I had begun on the bus ride to Memphis in June 1973: every detail of my time with him, which became rarer, of my fears and dreams, of my constant prayers. Not a day went by that I didn't record some aspect of my friendship with Elvis.

October 8, 1975

I have not heard from Elvis since that early morning call of September 20. No one has contacted me. I don't want to pester anyone for information, either; I'm not that close to the family to warrant that. I'm sure most of his friends merely tolerate me as it is. They sure won't share personal information with me.

As much as I respect Elvis's privacy, I long to know how he is doing and feeling. Has he gotten treatment for his addiction? I pray so. More than anything in this world, I want him healthy and well and happy. He deserves all of that and so very much more.

Until I know he is well, I know these nightmares will continue. They will, because I have no control over them and they come from the deepest part of me, the part that taps into things I cannot truly know otherwise. Being an empath and picking up on other people's pain and emotions is not always pleasant; it's draining and heavy. But the benefit is that I always know when people are dishonest about how they feel. Mom used to often say she felt fine, when I could literally feel her pain. It's the same with Elvis. Even though I never had a personal connection to him before 1973, I could feel his pain. I knew things were wrong with him. I still do. I can't, though, know for certain if he still takes the pills, and with his pre-existing hereditary conditions, I live in constant fear for his life. He was in part self-medicating as Mom had and in part addicted to certain drugs. The combination was, well, a prescription for disaster. How could it be stopped? How?

SSSSS

"Hello?"

"Caroline, this is Joe. Elvis wants you to come to the movies with us tonight. Be at Graceland around midnight. Okay?"

"Sure. Thanks for calling, and tell Elvis thanks, too." I hung up from the call, stunned. The invitation came out of nowhere, was totally unexpected, and was last minute—all completely, typically Elvis, and I felt elated. He was known for his spontaneity as much as for his generosity. No matter what else was going on with him, he remained the man-child I had come to know and to love dearly.

As promised, I arrived at the mansion at midnight, to be summarily ushered to Elvis's Lincoln for the drive to the theater, this time the Crosstown. Linda and the entourage also came, of course, and we all had a blast watching *One Flew Over the Cuckoo's Nest.*

I watched Elvis as much as I watched the film, and I could tell that he thoroughly enjoyed the story, which raised several issues that he questioned on the drive home.

Back at Graceland, Elvis, Linda, me, and some of the Memphis Mafia members sat around discussing the themes and actions depicted in the movie.

"What I want to know is, were people like McMurphy, Billy, and Chief really crazy, mentally ill? Why were they admitted to a mental hospital if they weren't?" one of the guys asked.

"No, none of them are crazy. They're sent there to subdue them, keep them in line, make them follow the established order of society," Elvis replied.

He continued, "Ratched versus the patients symbolizes the theme of repression versus expression. See, when people bring disorder into an orderly environment, this kind of power struggle ensues. Those in charge of that society, in this case the hospital staff, do all they can to repress the disorderly and to maintain the order. Look at what happened during the 60s, the hippie movement and the war protests. Same thing. When people protested, they were arrested or even killed. Maintain the status quo, the order at all costs."

I listened intently, amazed once again at Elvis's intelligence and deep thoughts. We continued to discuss the movie's themes, and one by one the guys each went to bed. I thoroughly relished this conversation, so reminiscent of that first night when I had to sit up with him. Elvis contained so many profound thoughts, more than most people would ever think about themselves or suspect that Elvis Presley pondered.

"You challenged the order in 1954. Some groups of people attempted to repress and silence you. Jesus challenged everyone and everything, and those in opposition to Him thought they had silenced Him. In both cases, the repression failed, just as it does in the movie. Billy frees himself through suicide. Chief Bromden frees McMurphy by suffocating him. Chief Bromden escapes.

"There is a way to challenge, to be disorderly, to shake things up, but it has to gain wide support, don't you think?" I asked.

"I think so," Linda said. "The more support a challenge to the established order has, the less it can be silenced. Take Dr. King. He may have been assassinated, but his movement had already garnered so much support that it was impossible to stop it or to silence it. His work still continues."

"Yeah. It takes a mighty person like Jesus or Martin Luther King to buck the established order. I admire both of those men tremendously, I do. There is so much to learn from them, I tell you. Both of them changed the world forever," Elvis added.

"So did you," I told him and smiled. "So did you."

§§§§§

After my Saturday, March 27, 1976 morning routine, I made tea and settled at my desk to read. My doorbell rang at 8:17, which surprised me; I never received many visitors. I ran downstairs, peered through the door's peephole and quickly flung open the door. "Marcus! What's wrong? Why are you here?"

"Nothing's wrong. Have you seen the morning paper?" He looked at me in confusion. "I said nothing's wrong. Don't look so scared. Here, look."

He had the page folded and thrust it at me. *Elvis Offers Assistance at Highway Traffic Accident* read the headline. The night before, as he drove along the highway, Elvis stopped at the scene of a serious vehicle accident, showed his police badge, and offered help. Photographs showed him getting out of his white Lincoln Continental wearing a red leather cape coat and signature sunglasses, smoking a slim cigar, as well as talking to police officers at the scene.

"See! Look! Elvis really is a superhero! He looks cooler than Batman or Superman, he has police badges, guns, knows karate, and helps people!" Marcus enthused in one breath.

My smile felt two miles wide. Elvis did look handsome, stylish, and more importantly, concerned and willing to help. "I know, Marcus. I know," I said and stared at the pictures. "He's the most amazing man I will ever meet."

Marcus cocked his head and touched my arm. "Does he know, Caroline?"

"Know what? That he's amazing? No, he's far too humble to think that, Marcus."

"No, not that. Does he know how much you really love him?"

"I tell him I love him every time I see him, so yes, I'd say he does," I replied and smiled at my young friend.

"No, not that kind of love. Does he know how you really feel about him?"

What? My father had said the same thing to me in late 1973. There was no use denying it any longer, not to myself or to anyone else. "I-I can't tell him that, sweetheart. I can't. He has a girlfriend, Linda, and I really like her, you know. I can't cause problems between them and me. Yes, I love him, but, honestly, Marcus, I'm more than grateful to be his friend."

"Yeah, if you say so. But one day your heart's gonna get broken real hard. He might not mean to, but he will hurt you somehow, someday. Who's gonna take care of you when he does?"

§§§§§

I went to the office as usual on an early spring Monday morning, in part to go over my case files and appointments for the day. As I sat at my desk reading files and making notes, one of my co-workers, Jane Staley, came over and said she had a favor to ask me.

I smiled and asked her what. Her response took me aback.

"I've lived here for years, you know, and, well, I'm a huge Elvis fan. I wonder if you can get me inside Graceland, you know, introduce me to him. That'd be just fabulous."

No one had yet asked me such a thing; if anyone had, they would have gotten the same answer I told Jane. I took a deep breath, looked her in the eyes, and firmly said, "I can't do that. It's not my place to bring strangers to his private home. Even I rarely go without an invitation. I refuse to take advantage of his kindness for any reason."

"What? Are you serious? All I want is to meet him, not marry him. Or is that what you're after? Fine, be stingy. Just don't ever ask me for any favors. You know what my answer will be." Jane stormed away in anger.

I knew she would talk about me, but I didn't care. God, Elvis, and I knew the truth. And, no, I would never abuse our friendship. Graceland was his one refuge from the outside world, and I would never dare invade that privacy for anyone. Even Marcus had never visited the mansion.

I continued to do my work, but now expected that some of my co-workers would make my life at the office as miserable as they could. Let them. I didn't get into this career for them; I became a social worker to help people overcome their problems. That's who and what I always focused upon, not being the most-liked in the office.

My day brightened when I received a telephone call from Joe. I spoke quietly, not wanting my side of the conversation overheard. Joe told me Elvis's summer concerts would soon be announced, and he wanted to give me an advanced notice.

"Your folks live in Philadelphia, right?" I told him they did. "Well, Elvis is performing there on June 28 at the Spectrum. I thought your parents would like to attend and meet him backstage before the show."

"Really? Joe, that's so kind! I'll call them after work and tell them to be ready when the tickets go on sale. They'll love meeting him!"

"They don't need to buy tickets. We always get some for friends and family. I'll have two left at will-call for them; arrange to meet them before the show so I can get you all backstage. We'll work out the details closer to the show."

"Thank you. And tell Elvis I love him for this. I'm donating the money they'd have spent on the tickets to St. Jude's in his name. It's the least I can do for all of his kindness. Thank you."

The rest of the day felt blissful. Nothing anyone at the office said or did could ever bother me. God continued to bless me, and my heart was too full of gratitude and happiness to feel upset by petty people.

I drove home as soon as work ended and called my parents. My father was still at work, so I gave Joe's news to Mom, who screamed so loud I thought she'd deafened my left ear.

"Is this really true? I'm going to meet Elvis? Really? This isn't some cruel joke?"

"No, Mom, it's not. It's true. You and Dad will meet Elvis before the concert that night. It might not be very long, but you will meet him. Bring something you'd like him to autograph, and bring your camera so you can get your picture taken with him. Who knows when this kind of opportunity will happen again?"

"Oh, thank you for reminding me! I need to buy lots of film for the camera, and choose my favorite record cover for him to sign. Oh, and I need to get a new outfit, something befitting the occasion. This doesn't happen every day, at least not for me and your father, it doesn't. It might for you, Caroline, but not for us. Oh, there's so much to do!"

I laughed. "Calm down, Mom. You've got more than two months before the concert. I just wanted to let you know so you two don't leave town or make other plans that night, that's all."

"So, you're coming home?"

"For a couple of days, yes. I spoke to my supervisor this afternoon, and I'm using two of my vacation days. It'll be a quick trip, but I'll be there. I'll call you soon, so I can talk to Dad, too. 'Bye."

§§§§§

I caught a flight to Philadelphia early on Monday, June 28, 1976. I couldn't take a chance there wouldn't be delays, so I booked the first flight of the day, which left at 5:10. I planned to spend the day with Mom while Dad went to work.

A taxi dropped me at my parents' home just after 8:00. I let myself in with my key, and quietly walked up behind Mom as she stood looking out the kitchen window. She jumped when I hugged her, and I laughed.

"I'm sorry, Mom, but I wanted to surprise you."

"You did," she said as she held her hand to her throat. "I have so much still left to do before tonight. I made an appointment at the beauty parlor to get my hair and nails done. That's at 11. Then I have to make sure there's film actually in the camera. I bought all this film just for tonight. Oh, I want a picture of you and Elvis together. We have to do that tonight if nothing else. Do you have any pictures of you and Elvis? You've never said."

I put my hands on her shoulders and smiled. She was more excited than a child on Christmas morning. "Calm down, Mom. There's plenty of time. Relax. Believe me, I know this is exciting, but we've got eleven hours yet. Oh, and no, I don't have an actual picture of us, just those from newspapers when I was in the group."

"Why ever not?"

"It just never entered my mind in the moment. You know, I was so wrapped up in our conversations that nothing else mattered. I have my memories and my diary. They're all I need."

"Well, you're getting one tonight. Your father will have to take it. My hands are already shaking."

I went with Mom to her appointment, and then treated her to lunch. We talked—not about Elvis—and laughed a lot. That felt wonderful; I hadn't laughed, really laughed, in so long. It seemed all of my tension evaporated.

Mom noticed through the façade, though. "What's been troubling you? It's him, isn't it?"

I tried to hedge the question, but she persisted. "What do you want me to say?" I asked in a veritable whisper. "Yes, I'm worried about him, just like Dad was worried about you when you were sick. That's all."

"That's all?" Mom whispered, too. "What is really going on between you two?"

"Mom! What do you think? We're friends, that's all. No matter what I feel, we'll remain friends."

"What do you mean 'no matter what I feel'? Just what do you feel, Caroline?"

I stared at my spaghetti and barely whispered, "I love him. With every molecule of my soul, I love him."

"Caroline. You're asking to get your heart broken, don't you realize that?"

I looked at my mother and firmly said, "Not by him. Never by him. He may never love me this way, I know that.

I'm okay with that. Linda is the best woman for him, and I hope they get married. I do. It's just that knowing him is far more spiritual than I ever expected it to be. I don't know how to explain it except to say that he fuels my brain and my soul. His thoughts, ideas, and questions bring truth, knowledge, wisdom, clarity to me. He is my spiritual guide."

"Caroline! Don't do that, not to him or to any man."

"Do what? Value and treasure his wisdom?"

"No. Don't turn him into God in your heart. He's not. He's a man, like your father and any of the men in here. Just a man, not perfect and with faults. Don't elevate him to godlike status. Don't."

"I haven't. Really. I'm well aware of his struggles. But it's all he does despite those issues that fills me with awe and gratitude. And fear. I'm afraid he's on a path toward something very serious. I don't know what to do. I've talked to him before, but that's not enough. I don't know what else to do."

"Is this related to the issue he and I had in common?" my mother asked. I knew she referenced the self-medicating. I nodded. "Pray. But you can't stop it or change it. Only he can, dear." She leaned closer so even her whisper wouldn't be overheard. "Addiction is a disease, just like cancer or emphysema, and only professional treatment can help. You know that. He should be in a clinic."

"I know. I encouraged him to get help, for his daughter if not for anyone else. I honestly think he tried, but I know him. He can't be forced into something, no matter what it is. He just won't be forced against his will."

"Do you realize what you just said? He isn't willing to change. Until he is, no one else can do anything to change his behavior."

"I know. I know this started early, but got worse after his mother's death. My honest take: this is his way to numb the pain so he can function. That, I totally get, Mom. He changed after his mother's death. He knows she's in Heaven, but they were so very close that he has to feel that part of him died with her, part of his spirit."

"I understand that, but he has a young daughter to think of now. He can't want her to go through what he's dealing with. Let's just pray that he finds the will to break free."

We spent the rest of the afternoon deliberately avoiding our lunchtime topic. I had to admit that I felt a release telling someone, someone I trusted and who wouldn't judge Elvis. I couldn't and wouldn't ever judge or condemn him; no one except him and God fully knew all that led and contributed to his drug abuse. I sure didn't, and I didn't need to know. I just needed and wanted him healthy.

Dad got home at 5:30, in time for supper and a shower before we had to leave for the Spectrum. Mom had bought a new dress—or should I say evening gown—for the event.

"You look like you're meeting the Queen, Norma," Dad teased her.

"Not quite. I'm meeting the King," she quickly replied with a sparkle.

"Don't call him that. He dislikes it, because Jesus is the King," I warned my parents as we got in Dad's car.

"I read that, now that you mention it," Dad commented. "Quite humble for someone of his stature."

"Isn't he?" I softly said from the back seat, not noticing the full import of the glance my parents exchanged.

When we arrived, the parking lot was filling, and we made our way to the will-call window for the tickets, which we quickly got and headed for the backstage area where I asked for Joe, who soon motioned us back.

"Elvis isn't here yet, but you can wait here. Help yourselves to some water and fruit."

Joe went to wait for Elvis and to make sure everything was on schedule. Mom mumbled, "I couldn't eat or drink anything right now without choking to death. I'm a nervous wreck."

I put my arm around her and smiled. "I know. I'd have been, too, if I'd met him under these circumstances."

"Yes, well, you certainly have a story to tell your grandchildren. Getting knocked down and out by Elvis Presley."

I smiled, but inwardly thought, *"I'll never have grandchildren, because I'm never getting married. My heart and soul belong to just one man. You both sense that, don't you? Don't expect me to follow that traditional path, because I can't. I can't betray my one true love. Don't ask me to. Please."*

About six minutes later, Elvis entered with some of his bodyguards, and Mom audibly gasped. Elvis looked in our direction and smiled. "Little Bit! You came!" he said and kissed me.

"Of course I did. I'm so happy to see you again," I said and hugged him.

"How have you been?" he asked me.

"Busy, but fine. You look wonderful."

He smiled but looked embarrassed. I knew the bloating made him self-conscious, but it never detracted from his physical and spiritual beauty in my eyes and mind.

"Elvis, I'd like you to meet my parents. My father, Harvey Hart, and my mother, Norma Hart."

"It's nice to meet you, Sir," Elvis said to my father and shook his hand. He turned to my mother and said, "It's a real pleasure to meet you, Mrs. Hart. I see where your daughter gets her beauty." The cherry on the sundae was the kiss on her cheek.

My mother suddenly resembled the teenybopper I'd seen in old pictures, swooning and appearing that she would faint.

"It's totally my pleasure, Your Maj—Mr. Presley," Mom managed to say, catching her faux pas just in time.

Elvis laughed, which filled my heart with joy; his laugh always did. "Elvis; please call me Elvis. There's no need to be so nervous around me. We're like old friends, you know. I've known your little girl for three years now, saw her get through graduate school and become a fine social worker. She does a lot of good for the people of Memphis. You two must be proud."

"We are, Elvis, very proud. Caroline is a fine young lady," Dad said. This must be what it feels like when parents show their children's baby pictures. My cheeks felt hot, and I knew I was blushing. "Seems my little girl has something in common with you. You two would make a perfect pair."

"Oh? What's that?" Elvis asked.

"Humility. She's blushing."

"I hate to interrupt, but before you have to go, would you mind signing this album cover for me? Please?" Mom asked, saving me from further embarrassment.

"Why, sure." He asked for a pen, and personalized a message to Mom on the cover of his first album, *Elvis Presley*, released when I was not yet two years old.

Dad asked if he and Mom could have their picture taken with Elvis, which I took, and then Mom did indeed say, "I want a picture of you and Caroline together."

"Come here, Little Bit," Elvis said with a smile, and I stood closer to him. He put an arm around me, and I put one arm around him and the other hand on his arm. I never knew exactly when Dad snapped the picture, for I was besotted with Elvis and staring at him the entire time. "Give me a copy of that, will you,

Little Bit?" Elvis asked and kissed me again as he got ready to go on stage. We were quickly rushed to our front-row seats.

The concert opened strong, with his iconic songs and moves, and only soared higher as it progressed. Every chance to see him perform was a gift and treasure for me, and I watched and listened attentively, intending to preserve the moments in my diary.

There were some once-in-a-lifetime memories that night. Nearly halfway through the show, Elvis looked down at me and sang one of the most poignant songs he had recorded, *And I Love You So*. I stared at him, once more smitten by his vocal depth, power, and emotion, as well as his sheer beauty. "Surely, Adonis was not as beautiful."

"What did you say?" my father asked me as he leaned very close.

"Huh? Oh, he's gorgeous."

"You didn't say it quite like that." He leaned close to my mother and repeated my Adonis comment. Had I said it aloud? She shushed him, thankfully.

Near the end of the concert, he did a new song he had recorded in February at Graceland, *Hurt*. The power in his voice and the emotions in his delivery brought me to tears—literally. I could not stop crying, my own emotions on overdrive.

When the song ended, a scarf landed in my lap. I looked up at him through my tears, and he motioned for me to dry my tears. Instead, I clutched the sweat-soaked scarf to my chest, yet another token of our friendship I would cherish for the rest of my life.

I leapt to my feet in a standing ovation when the concert ended and he walked the edge of the stage. He bent down in front of me and beckoned me to him for a kiss.

"I love you," I said before he stood, and he flashed the sign language of the sentiment. I clutched that as tightly as I did the scarf.

"That was quite some concert," Mom said in the car on the drive home. "His voice is stronger and richer than ever."

"Yes," Dad agreed. "It was a very interesting concert. Wasn't it, Caroline?"

"Uh-huh, just perfect," I said in a day-dreamy tone.

The magic didn't fade by the time my father drove me to the airport the following morning. I held my purse tightly against me in the car; my prized scarf was safely wrapped in a silk handkerchief inside, along with the ticket stub.

My father made small talk until we sat in the lounge awaiting my boarding call. Then he opened up. "That really was some show last night, both before and during the concert."

I looked at him, shock plain on my face. "What's that supposed to mean?"

"It's no secret how you feel about him. You've told me and your mother and him. He knows. He also knows you'll always be there no matter what. Those looks you shot his way all night said it more than words ever could. He knows he's got a trustworthy, reliable friend. He gave you special attention last night. He singled you out. He cares for you, too. I just wonder if—well, if he might have you waiting in the wings when it's time for the next girlfriend. You know that will hurt you, because he's not a one-woman man. That's when you'll get hurt."

"Dad, I'm not his next girlfriend, believe me. We're friends; we have a spiritual connection. He doesn't have romantic feelings for me. He likes me, and yes, he loves me, but not that way. That's definitely one-sided on my side. I've said it before. I told Mom today at lunch. I love him with all of my soul. I want him to be healthy and happy. That's all. I'll never be in league with his girlfriends."

"Why not? What would stop you?"

"First, I didn't go to Memphis and want to see him with that in mind. It never entered my thoughts, ever. He's not going to marry again, I sense that. He craves love, attention, and a mother figure. Linda provides all of that. I could, too, of course, but I won't. He doesn't see me that way. Besides, I couldn't live with any man unless I was married to him. I love him. I would marry him. But he's never going to ask me, so it's a mute point. I will always be there for him, and I will always love him more than I will ever love another. Okay?"

My father hung his head as my flight was called and I rushed to board and return to my life in Memphis.

§§§§§

One week later, Elvis ended his tour by performing an Independence Day concert at Memphis's Mid-South Coliseum. I once more witnessed his stupendous talent, which I again recorded in my diary that night.

July 6, 1976

Memphis didn't need fireworks to continue America's Bicentennial celebration. We had Elvis tonight! He lit up the coliseum with that voice, charm, and always heart-stopping beauty. He really is the one most beautiful human being I have ever seen in photographs, paintings, films, books, art—simply stunning.

More than his physical beauty, though, is his spiritual, soul, beauty. Despite his heath issues and drug addiction, he remains the most compassionate, charitable, faithful man I ever knew. Plus, he has a wicked sense of humor, and it showed itself a few times tonight. He was genuinely happy tonight, and everyone felt that. I felt his happiness, and his happiness fills me with joy. I pray he will feel that all of the time.

He wore the same jumpsuit he wore in Philadelphia, and both times he looked just fabulous. I know he's ill, but that doesn't detract from his beauty or my perception of it. Neither does his illness make him less of a performer. On the contrary, it deepens my love and respect for him.

For him to put aside his ego and stand in front of millions of people a year, bloated and more limited in movement, hurts my heart for him, but more than that makes me realize just how dedicated he is and how much he works to please people.

But he shouldn't be performing at all. He should have at least one year off to devote to taking care of himself. He spends all of his energy taking care of others, providing for others. That alone is, I know, a big part of the drug abuse. He feels he has to keep going no matter how he feels, and it's destroying his health.

I wish I could whisk him away where his 'people' can't find him, somewhere he can get the treatment and rest he needs. I'm going to talk to him about this. It's his life, contracts or not, and he needs to save it before it's too late. We'll go to

*another country using pseudonyms and fake IDs.
I'll have Dad get them for us. I have to do this.
I have to. It's the only way to save him.*

SSSSS

Unfortunately, I hadn't found a chance to talk to Elvis alone since the July 5 concert, and it was already fall. I had hoped to have our plan formulated by now. I knew I could rely on Dad to help us; he knew a pilot who could get us out of the country. It would work, but I needed Elvis's participation. I knew he had a spontaneous, adventurous spirit; he just didn't get to express it often. I knew the whole secret mission aspect of our get-away would appeal to his comic book and action movie loving nature. Finding the opportunity to talk to him completely alone was the first major obstacle.

When my phone rang late on October 29, I knew it was Elvis, and I grabbed the handset. "Elvis?"

"How'd you know, Little Bit? ESP?" he joked.

"Not really. Not many people call me after ten. Is everything okay?"

"Yeah, sure. I just want you to come over for a while. I'm in my bedroom. Come on up when you get here. I'll be waiting."

I quickly put on my coat, grabbed my purse, and drove to Graceland. No one questioned or tried to stop me when I headed upstairs; he must have alerted them I was coming. I knocked on his door and entered to find him sitting on his bed.

"You look happy. What's been going on?" I asked.

"Come with me," he said. I followed him through his large master bathroom into his dressing room. I was flabbergasted; it was a converted bedroom. A bed actually stood against the front wall, which he explained was for a bodyguard's use. Two separate wardrobes contained clothes I had seen in films such as *That's the Way It Is* and in photographs and over the past three years—plus many more pieces and outfits I had never seen.

"This is amazing! I know some women who would do almost anything for a closet like this."

"A lot of this stuff is old. It's time to purge." He looked through the racks for a few moments and removed a silk, flower-print shirt. He held it up to me. "You can have it altered. Here," he said and draped the shirt over my arm.

"What are you doing? You can't give away your clothes."

"Sure, I can. I've already given a bunch to the singers and musicians, just tokens. Now it's your turn. I want you all to have these, so don't say no please."

I knew better by now than to argue or to protest. But I had to tell him, "I don't need things and gifts from you, Elvis. I just need you happy and healthy. I wanted to talk to you, so I'm glad you called. I have an idea." I told him my plan, everything I had thought out. "It's perfect. With disguises and fake IDs, including passports, no one will easily find us. And my father's pilot friend is trustworthy; he will get us somewhere safe. You need time to rest and get the proper medical treatment. This is the only way. Please come away for a while. Please."

He listened, and I could see in his eyes that the idea appealed to him. I was sure he would tell me to put the plans in motion.

"That's very sweet of you, Little Bit, it really is. I'd love to get away from the grind and constant work, but I can't. Too many people depend on me. My payroll is enormous. I can't just up and disappear no matter how tempting that sounds."

"You have to. You're working yourself to death, don't you see that? I love you too much to let you do that. Please go away for a while. Please." Tears filled my eyes and blurred my vision.

"I love you for thinking of this, I do. This isn't the right time. Next year we'll do this, I promise. In one year, we'll sneak off somewhere, and I promise I'll get treatment and rest. One year. I promise."

"I'll hold you to that promise, you know that. No excuses on October 29, 1977. No excuses. Clear?"

"Sure, Little Bit. You've got my word."

VERSE THREE:
AMAZING GRACE

I dropped off my gift and card on Elvis's 42nd birthday, but I didn't see him. He didn't perform in Vegas as he usually did at the beginning of the year, and I worried that he was ill. Despite his promise to go away at the end of October, I feared that was too long to wait. He desperately needed help.

My daily and nightly prayers continued, and the nightmares returned. And with no sight or word from him since Christmas, my fears increased despite my attempts to dampen them.

Then I made the mistake of opening the evening *Memphis Press Scimitar* newspaper on Friday, April 1, 1977. A headline froze me: *Elvis Admitted to Baptist*

Memorial Hospital. No! I scanned the article, and honestly didn't know whether to believe it or not. *"Entertainer Elvis Presley was admitted to Baptist Memorial Hospital early today after canceling a show at the last minute in Baton Rouge, La., and flying to Memphis with complaints of intestinal flu."* He did have intestinal issues, serious issues, so intestinal flu would only exacerbate them, I attempted to rationalize.

I prayed around the clock, silently in my head when at work—even during meetings and presentations—and out loud at home. I sat up most nights, afraid of the nightmares and their dark messages of impending doom.

I didn't go to Graceland; there was no need with him not there. He and Linda had broken up before Christmas, and she wouldn't be with him. He already had a new girlfriend, one I had briefly met and didn't yet get to know in the slightest. Everything was changing in his world, and I wasn't convinced the changes were for the best.

I understood why Linda had to leave; she had dealt with his drug addiction first-hand and had seen all it was doing to him. The stress was too great. I couldn't blame her. I know they loved each other still and always would. I just wondered if Linda's absence was one reason for his recent decline. She had been such a strong force in his life, but as my mother had told me, no one person could save him. To expect Linda to do so was extremely unfair to her.

Some good news appeared in the April 6 *Commercial Appeal*, the headline of which announced *Elvis at Home: Hospital on Call*. The story went on to report that he had been "*released at 4 AM [the previous morning, although] He decided to keep the rooms reserved [and that] he is feeling fine and looking forward to returning to his personal appearance tours that begin April 21 at Greensboro, NC.*"

I prayed he was all right; he must be for the doctors to release him. I made that my mantra, reminding myself that no doctor would release him if he were ill, no matter how much he demanded or threatened. I had to trust that the doctors at BMH did the best and right treatment possible for Elvis. I had to, otherwise I would fall apart.

He did resume his tour, and was on the road from April 21 through May 3—not too long, thankfully. However, after a short break, he did another tour beginning May 20 and scheduled to end on June 2.

I received another call from Joe regarding a May 28 concert once more at Philadelphia's Spectrum. My parents and I were again provided tickets and a meeting with Elvis before the show.

As I had the previous year, I flew to Philadelphia early on May 28 and this time spent the week with both of my parents, as Dad had taken the week off as a vacation. They had encouraged me to also take the week off so that I could stay with them and spend quality time with them.

We arrived at the Spectrum to an already packed parking lot, but since we were meeting Elvis backstage before the show, I knew we had plenty of time. Joe found chairs for us, but I couldn't sit. I just needed to see Elvis.

"Elvis concerts are becoming a regular part of your life, Caroline," Mom commented.

"What? Well, I have attended far more of them than I ever dreamed I would, that's true. But I don't take any concert for granted. Each one is a beautiful gift I will treasure all of my life. I left here almost four years ago, praying to see him just once. My life has been a dream-come-true since then."

As Joe rushed by me, he smiled and said, "You need to tell him that. He's coming in."

"You've got it hard," Dad said. "Your eyes are already lit up and he's not here yet. Wrong. I see he just appeared," he whispered, referencing my love-struck expression.

Elvis looked bloated, but happy and in upbeat spirits. I could tell that he was tired, even though he appeared resplendent in a white and gold jumpsuit.

Elvis smiled and hugged me. As I held him, I whispered, "Let's go away now. Let's just go. Your fans will understand. They want you healthy. Please."

Elvis pulled away and looked down at me. "October. I promised you October. Don't worry, Little Bit, I'll keep my promise to you."

He turned and greeted my parents, and they chatted for several minutes. When Joe came for Elvis, we were taken to our seats by a security guard.

"What's happening in October? You two planning a secret wedding?"

"Dad!   I'll tell you everything tomorrow.   We're going to need your help. No more here," I whispered in his ear.

Dad stared at me intently, a look of warning and worry on his face.   I wasn't sure that would go away the following day.

I focused on the stage as the lights dimmed and the *2001* theme began. Then he appeared, and my hands instantly went to my chest. "Oh, Elvis, I love you," I said. My father stared at me even more attentively.

I looked only at Elvis throughout the concert, never glancing at anyone or anything else. I truly prized each second in his presence; each was priceless. I had never dared dream of more than a few minutes with him. To be his friend was a far greater gift than I felt I deserved, yet I remained eternally grateful to God for aligning our paths that afternoon four years earlier.

I saw him look at me and see my expression, the love that surely shone from within me, the depth of my feelings for him. He smiled at me and tossed his scarf at me, his way of telling me he knew and understood. One more precious symbol of our soul connection and friendship.

I don't remember walking out of the Spectrum and getting in Dad's car or going in the house. I don't remember how I got in my old room—which hadn't been changed. The first thing I remembered was Mom's voice behind me.

"Do you want us to order a pizza? You barely ate anything before we left."

I shook my head, orienting myself, and said, "Oh, no. I can't eat."

"Why ever not? Are you sick?" she asked and put her hand on my forehead.

"No, I'm not sick. I'm just—just too overcome, too full of emotions. I just want to be alone for a while, please."

"I know what you told me, but you can't devote your life. . . ."

"Norma, I need your help in the kitchen. Now," Dad said. Bless him. He understood that I just needed to be alone and subsume the evening. Even though I had known Elvis for nearly four years, seeing him on stage, such a powerful, dynamic performer even as ill as he was, filled me with wonder, awe, and, well, a sort of disbelief.

These exceptional experiences made me doubt his existence. I mean, he was so beautiful, so commanding, so mesmerizing, that I wondered if I had imagined him, created him like an author creates a novel character. How could someone that spectacular be real? How?

Yet, my brain knew I had sat and talked with him, had touched him, had kissed him. I knew, intellectually, that he was real, but there were these moments when even my brain doubted the reality of my experiences with him. I had to have imagined him. "No one is that perfect."

"No one is perfect, baby, not even Elvis Presley," Dad said in a gentle, soft tone and put his hands on my shoulders. "He'd be the first to tell you that. Right?"

I nodded and softly replied, "He told me that the first night when we sat up talking for hours. It's just. . . . I don't know how to explain it."

"You don't have to explain it, not to me or to anyone. No human being is perfect, not me, not your mother, not Elvis. No one. He is a very generous, caring man, a very talented man, a very handsome man. He is, undeniably. But like all of us, he has his faults and flaws. I hear he has a pretty good temper, for one."

I giggled. "Fierce is how I describe it. But that's just because. . . ."

Dad put his finger over my lips, shushing me. "Don't make excuses for his faults, just accept them. Love him in spite of them. He is who he is."

"I know, Dad, and I do accept him as he is. Remember that song I said I liked? I love him and the life he lives. I don't have to agree with everything he does, but I know it's all part of him. I don't want to change him; I want to help him with some of his weaknesses." I went to make sure the bedroom door was closed. "Dad, can I talk to you now instead of tomorrow?"

"Sure, Kitten. I'm ready when you want to talk. I'll listen."

I told him my plan to secret Elvis to a European country for rest and treatment, every detail. "I have to do this, Dad, I have to. No one around him is doing anything. He's going on these endless tours, when he should be in a clinic or a hospital. I can't stand by and do nothing. This is the only way. That's what I whispered to him backstage, to just go with us, to leave with us."

My father paced around the room for several minutes before he spoke. I knew he was thinking through the plan and its logistics and risks. "This could work, but it has to be carefully arranged. October, huh? We've got time to get the pieces all in place. I'll talk to Michael, my pilot friend, and also Fred, my policeman friend. I won't tell them who yet, just that it's someone very important who needs help for drug addiction. We'll work it out, Caroline. We have time to think of the best way to get him in the plane."

"I've already thought of that. I'll have him pick me up at my house on a motorcycle, and we'll drive to the airport. Michael's plane will be waiting there.

Before we leave my house, we'll put on the wigs and disguises, then get on the plane. Michael can get us to Switzerland. We'll come back after his treatment, no matter how long it takes."

"People will have searches out for him immediately. There's going to be a high risk of you two getting caught."

"Not if we are father and daughter going on vacation. I'll work it all out, Dad. Every detail. This is the only way he'll ever get the drug abuse treatment that he desperately needs. I have to do this. I have to. The alternative is just too dreadful, Dad," I said and cried in his arms.

§§§§§

Elvis had a short break between tours, June 2 through June 16. I worked, still enjoying my clients, many of whom became friends, and the challenges. The people in the office never gave me a hard time or asked for special favors with Elvis. For whatever reason, the entire issue blew over, for which I was grateful.

I still saw Marcus, now 17 and soon to be a senior in high school. He still took karate lessons, and often told me how he and his friends hung around outside Graceland for a glimpse of their hero, Elvis. He was such a smart, handsome boy, and I knew Elvis would be proud of him.

One evening, as I sat in the upstairs office working on the escape plan, I heard what sounded like a motorcycle engine in my driveway. I raced down the stairs and flung the door open. It was!

"Hop on, Little Bit. Let's go for a ride."

"Let me get my keys and lock the door, and I'll be right there."

I ran like a frantic chicken, making sure I didn't keep him waiting long. He'd get mobbed if the neighbors saw him sitting there. I rushed to the motorcycle, and for the first time in my natural-born life, I got on a motorcycle—with Elvis!

He drove down the residential streets of my neighborhood until he finally got to Poplar Avenue. He drove for some time, not seeming to have any agenda, until he finally ended up on Elvis Presley Boulevard and went to his mansion.

As he turned toward the gates, the crowds gathered outside them swarmed him, screaming his name, taking pictures, and trying to run after him as he drove up the driveway. He parked under the carport and helped me off.

"Wanna go for a different kind of ride?" he asked.

I had no idea what he meant, but I didn't care. He was active and having fun—with me—and that's all that mattered to me. "Sure."

He took my hand and led me to the stables, where he had Rising Sun and Ebony's Double saddled. He helped me atop Ebony's Double, a beautiful black Tennessee Walking horse, while he mounted Sun, as he called his favorite horse.

He spurred Sun into a full run, and I had no choice but to urge Ebony's Double to catch up. We ran the horses for several minutes, then slowed them to a trot before he sped off again onto the front lawn. Ebony's Double and me followed, and soon, I realized Elvis was near the wall—and so did the fans on the other side of the wall.

He shook hands, signed autographs, chatted, and let people pet Sun. People clamored for his attention. Most of them had their cameras and took dozens of pictures of him and his handsome horse. I didn't realize right away that many people also took my picture, simply because I was with Elvis. I understood how they felt; they admired him, and they wanted to have their moments with him. After all, that's all I had dreamed of when I came to Memphis. I could have been one of them, I thought, and then looked at Elvis. *Thank you, God, for this blessing. You know what my friendship with Elvis means to me. Please protect him. October is still four months away. Please protect him.*

§§§§§

Elvis left for another tour on June 17 and returned to Graceland on the 27th. At least these recent tours hadn't been very long, I thought, and literally thanked God for that.

I saw him a few of times. We laughed, talked, joked, discussed Bible verses, and prayed. Lisa was staying with him, and the two clearly adored one another. She was adorable, with her father's eyes and smile, and I liked her very much.

Once, when Elvis had to tend to something, Lisa and I played dolls, which I enjoyed. As another only child, I never had sisters (or brothers) with whom to play. I adored children, and I often got on my knees to play with them. It was fun for me, too.

My visits with him during those times were unfortunately infrequent, for his girlfriend Ginger lived at Graceland and naturally desired to spend time with Elvis. I couldn't blame her, although I admitted to my diary that I wished I could talk to him alone again. However, I knew the chances of that were nonexistent unless he came to my house—another unlikely happening with Ginger and Lisa there. I had to content myself with the brief visits I did have with him, knowing I was blessed to have those visits no matter how short.

He looked tired but happy, and I knew without doubt that Lisa's presence was the cause of his happiness. He loved her, doted on her, and did anything for her. She, like I, was indeed a Daddy's Girl of the highest order. I could and would never resent or demy his cherished time with his daughter.

The summer of 1977 passed into August, and my life continued its usual routines of work, dropping cookies off for Uncle Vester—which I had done weekly for years—reading, and praying for Elvis.

Thankfully, my nightmares about him had subsided. However, I finalized my plans for the end of October. I called my father and went over them with him, and he informed me that the fake IDs and passports had been obtained. I was elated. This would happen. Elvis would receive the rest and treatment his body needed. He would become healthier.

Everything was going well, just as I had prayed it would. I just needed time alone with Elvis to go over the plan with him and make sure he would keep his promise.

On August 14, I drove to a florist shop and got a lovely bouquet of red and white roses, which I took with me to Forest Hill Cemetery. I walked to Gladys Presley's grave, which was guarded by a stunning marble statue of Jesus.

"Mrs. Presley, I wish I had the chance to know you. You are a very special woman. Elvis loves you more than he will ever love anyone else. He misses you. You are his whole world. I know God has His reasons for everything, but I wish you were here with your son now. He needs you more than ever. You could help him. Please somehow get the message to him that he must keep his promise to go away with me in October. Please. I'm so sorry for all the sadness you did have," I said aloud as I stood before her grave.

I knelt to place the roses on her grave, and jumped when I heard, "I'll keep my promise, Little Bit. For Lisa, for Mama, for my family, for you. You know, Mama always worried that I wasn't taking care of myself. I guess she'd be very worried now, huh? I'll do better, I promise. The end of October. We'll go over the plans, okay?"

Tears of gratitude filled my eyes as I looked at him, handsome as always in a blue shirt and pants and holding a white basket of blue carnations.

"I just wanted to pay my respects to your mother and, well, I guess you heard. I needed to talk to her. I hope you don't mind."

"Nah. She would have liked you a lot, Little Bit. Just like I do."

"Thank you. I know I'd love her. Just like I love you. I do love you, Elvis. I'll leave you alone with her."

He took my hand as I started to walk away. "I love you, too, Caroline," he said to me with deep feeling in his voice for the first time.

§§§§§

As I drove back to my office after a meeting with a client in her home, I saw an ambulance speed down Elvis Presley Boulevard toward his mansion. NO! my brain screamed. I drove quickly to Graceland, where those gathered were frantic. I could see the ambulance in the distance, near the front entrance. Dr. Nichopoulos sped through the gates. I knew.

I couldn't move. I stood, numb and stunned, as the ambulance raced out of the gates and toward Baptist Memorial Hospital. I knew. I stood there, unable to cry, unable to move, unable to breathe.

"Caroline! What's going on?!" someone screamed and grabbed me.

I looked at the person, and suddenly my body snapped back to life. "Marcus. Oh, Marcus," I said and put a hand on his cheek. Then the tears came.

"No, Caroline, no! No!"

"Marcus. Come with me," I said and led him to my car—the car Elvis had bought me in 1973. We got in, and sat silent and still for several minutes, the shock fresh and raw.

I started the car and drove to my house—the house Elvis had bought me. I went straight to the telephone and dialed my father's private work number. When he answered, all I could say was, "Dad, Elvis is dead."

POSTLUDE:
MEMORIES

August 16, 1977

Elvis, I love you more than ever. I believe you know that. I wonder what you think of the world now. You said the world would change after you left it, and it has, more than anyone in 1977 could have ever imagined, not my parents, not me, not you. It's not always pretty down here, you know. So much has changed.

But so much is the same, my love. Memphis is packed with upwards of 60,000 people here to celebrate you. You thought you'd be forgotten, and no matter how much we all told you that you could never be forgotten, you never believed us. You were always so humble. The greatest man in the world, and so humble. I love you for that.

I love you for so much, for so many reasons. I love you. I miss you several times each day. I wish I could talk to you so often, about so many things. I wish so much had been different, but it wasn't, and there's nothing I can do about that.

I do know that in His way, God saved you from further suffering and illness. I prayed for Him to protect you, and like the loving Father He is, He did that. I never wanted you to die. I never wanted to live a life without you in it. Oh, if only we had gone away as we planned, everything. . . .

No. That won't do any good. The past is past, and there is no rewrite. We didn't get to go away to Switzerland. Destiny didn't allow that. But your destiny placed you on God's path, and your legacy has remained strong and vibrant.

I told you on June 6, 1973 that God had a purpose for you—to bring people to God, to evangelize for Him, to affect people, to change people. You do, still. I see it. I hear about it. So many people have shared their stories of how you changed them for the better. You, my love, continue to do God's work.

I also told you that first night that God revealed to me that you were an angel. Well, you are; you always were. He called you back to your eternal home in Heaven. God knew what I knew, that this world was too much for you. He saw and felt your suffering and conflicts while you walked this planet and did His work. He knew, and He ended your suffering the only way He could. He took you home.

I know you can see all on this earth. You can see me now, still in the house you bought for me forty-four years ago. I told you and my parents I would never leave this house, and I haven't. I won't. I want to die in this house, my gift from you.

The Cadillac you gave me stays in my garage. I start the engine and drive it down the street every once in a while. I drove it for many years, but I didn't want too much wear and tear on it, so like an old racehorse, it's retired. I'll keep it forever. Well, for the rest of my life anyway. It's in my will that it gets donated to the Graceland car museum when I die.

So do the scarves and shirt you gave me go on permanent loan to Graceland. They were yours, from you, and they should be returned to your home. Oh, I'm sure you know it's been a museum for many years now. I've never gone on a tour. I prefer my memories of my visits there. I'm sure you understand that.

You also know I've never had a serious relationship with any man. People often ask me why I've never dated. I prefer not to tell them.

But you know the reason, don't you? You. I meant it when I said you are the greatest love of my life. I could never love another man, not the way I love you. I could never be in a serious relationship with and marry another man when I love you so very much. It wouldn't be fair to the other man or to me. Or to our friendship and your memory. You spoiled me for other men.

I'm sure you and my parents often watch me with a combination of pride and bemusement. I'm also sure my parents would like to lecture me at times, even at my age. I'd like to think so. I miss them, too, very much.

Despite the empty hole in my heart for the past forty years, my life is good, and I am fine. I know you are alive and vibrant in Heaven, singing with the angel choir and making music with your friends. How I look forward to our heavenly reunion when God decides my life on earth is done and I have done my duty. That moment, when I feel your tender hands on mine once more, will be the culmination of my life's greatest desire.

Until then, may God keep you. I love you, Elvis.

Sheilah R. Craft is an English professor, writer, blogger, poet, artist, ardent genealogist, and book lover. Born and raised in the Midwestern United States, Sheilah was born surrounded by a close family—including several educators—books, and animals. She began reading and writing very early, and has published novels, short stories, articles, and poems. She was literally born a writer. Her series of novels centered on the lives of one family dynasty and spanning more than two centuries began in the fall of 2012 with the first volume, *Heart-Glow: A Novel.* Sheilah has written and had published one or two novels or books per year since then.

Published by STARLIGHT Books:

•HEART-GLOW: A NOVEL

•FIRST LOVE NEVER DIES: HEART-GLOW VOLUME II

•HEART ETERNAL: HEART-GLOW VOLUME III

•LIFE ETERNAL: HEART-GLOW VOLUME IV

•THE SPLENDOR OF HEAVEN BY SAINT ANGILIA: HEART-GLOW VOLUME V

• HEARTSONG SONATA

•MARY MAGDALENE: A MYSTERY PLAY

Published by Little Butterfly:

•THE QUEST FOR PERFECTION: SHELLEY AND THE POET-HERO

•A DAY WITH TEDDY BEAR